I AM LUCIFER

JJ Liniger

Copyright © 2017 JJ Liniger
All rights reserved.
No part of this book may be reproduced in any form or by any electronic or mechanical means including information storage and retrieval system, without permission in writing from the author. The only exception is by a reviewer, who may quote short excerpts in a review.

This is a work of fiction. Names, characters, places and incidents either are products of the author's imagination or are used fictitiously. Any resemblance to actual events or locales or persons, living or dead, is entirely coincidental.

ISBN-10:1979254257
ISBN-13:978-1979254250

Scripture quotations are taken from the *Holy Bible,* King James Version. Public Domain.

NIV: Scripture taken from THE HOLY BIBLE, NEW INTERNATIONAL VERSION, NIV Copyright 1973, 1978, 1984, 2011 by Biblica, Inc. Used by permission. All rights reserved worldwide.

Lewis, C.S. 1943. *The Screwtape Letters.*

DEDICATION

This book is dedicated to my church family starting at Melanie Park Baptist church leading me to Capitan, New Mexico, then to Siloam Springs Bible church, Countryside Baptist church in Stillwater, and finally to Fellowship Bible Church.

Each Bible study and community group has placed a building stone, leading to the creation of this story. I hope you all will enjoy the journey and pray God uses this for His kingdom!

CONTENTS

I AM	1
LUCIFER	1
ACKNOWLEDGMENTS	7
CHAPTER ONE	9
CHAPTER TWO	23
CHAPTER THREE	32
CHAPTER FOUR	48
CHAPTER FIVE	58
CHAPTER SIX	68
CHAPTER SEVEN	78
CHAPTER EIGHT	91
CHAPTER NINE	103
CHAPTER TEN	111
CHAPTER ELEVEN	125
CHAPTER TWELVE	133
CHAPTER THIRTEEN	143
CHAPTER FOURTEEN	155
CHAPTER FIFTEEN	163
CHAPTER SIXTEEN	176
CHAPTER SEVENTEEN	186
CHAPTER EIGHTEEN	195
Dear Reader	205
Discussion Guide	216
Sneak Preview Of	220
God's Will	220
ABOUT THE AUTHOR	225

ACKNOWLEDGMENTS

Thank you to my awesome husband, patient children and loving family, I could not have done this without your support.

To great Pre-Readers, Crossroads Writing Group, Creative Writing Master Mind Facebook Group, NaNoWriMo and 20booksto50k Facebook Group you have all encouraged me through this journey.

Thank you to Rita and Chris at rita_best on fiverr for editing, to ZERIG for the use of the cover graphic and to the hundreds of cover tutorials that helped me to produce this beautiful cover.

CHAPTER ONE

In the beginning God created the heavens and the Earth.
- Genesis 1:1 (KJV)

Darkness surrounded me. I drifted in emptiness through the beating of unseen wings lifting and lowering on my back. My breath quickened. I did not know where or who I was. My eyes strained to see into the blackness of nothing. Within the gloom, the sound of running water hastened my rapid breathing. I wasn't alone. My wings fluttered pulling me toward the sound. I had no control, but felt at peace.

From above a gray Cloud hovered, providing a soft glow. Water flowed and whirled in a circular motion around a large orb. Something kept the liquid from falling. Curiously I watched the Spirit traveled the circumference of the flowing ball and realized the radiant cloud was a Being, but not like me.

It was something bigger, grander, yet somehow whole and complete. From the Fog, hands gathered water and formed the fluid into a solid red sphere half the size of the original orb.

"What is that?" I asked.

The planet Mars, answered a voice in my mind.

I didn't know who replied, but felt at peace which resulted in me trusting the voice.

The Cloud threw the circle deep into the darkness. Maybe, the Fog didn't like what it had made. The Creator formed another blue ball. I gasped as the planet grew over four times the size of the original sphere. Certainly, this magnitude would please the Maker. Again, the orb was tossed out into the night.

The hands formed another planet in equal size of the original, but the Spirit discarded that ball to the darkness, along with three smaller ones. The Maker must be particular with its creation; each sphere appeared different from the other, but were equally spectacular.

This Thing could create, and I immediately became entranced in wonder. Did I have this same ability? I thought for a moment, but saw nothing that needed to be added.

I felt certain the Maker to be boastful when the Spirit brought out rings to surround the second largest planet. I had to move further back to avoid being caught in the planet's orbit.

"That's amazing," someone mumbled next to me.

"Truly," I responded.

An arch of gold outlined his wavy brown hair, which fell to his shoulders. His wings stretched as wide as his height. From the glow of the Fog, I saw gold along the perimeter of each feather throughout his wings and the lining of his breastplate and pants. Did I look the same? Specks of gold reflected off my white tunic which covered one shoulder and came down my legs in thick, white strips.

Too curious to stop, I touched the rings, outlining the planet. The band was cold and wet.

"Careful, friend," another angel said. His wings rose twice the length of his body. Each feather grew thicker, the largest being the same width as my hand. He wore strong muscles in place of a shirt and a white kilt came to his knees.

"What are you called?" I asked.

"I do not know," he answered.

The other angel gave me the same response which made sense, because I didn't know my name either. They probably guessed as much. In their silence, they appeared wise. I needed to remember their example.

I brought my hand out of the ring as a foreign particle passed. In total, the Maker created two spheres plus the one covered in water and then five more planets further out.

A voice called out. "Let there be light!"

From above, a blast of luminescence broke through the darkness. Beams splintered in all directions bringing with them boiling heat. Sterilizing fire covered the Earth.

I shielded my eyes from the brightness. What was this? Maybe it should be 'Who'.

Who has power to create with His voice?

I trembled, and my knees buckled. Had I been standing, I would have found myself kneeling, but somehow hovering in the air my body bent in the same position.

On either side of me, wings of various size and shape flapped, keeping the multitudes a float. Millions bowed their heads, and I did the same.

The Fog left the watery planet and floated toward the great light.

"Should we also go?" the shirtless one asked.

Wanting to appear brave, I nodded and followed the translucent cloud. I kept a safe distance but led the way as thousands of angels followed behind me.

We flew upward until level with the outer perimeter. I tried to guess the size of the palace, but there appeared to be no end to the light. Solid gold walls aligned the building. The structure grew higher and wider with each thick layer. The splendor of the castle made the creation of the planets pale in comparison.

Along the golden wall, I read: El Shaddai, Adonai, Yahweh, Jehovah, Shalom, Creator, Elohim, Abba-Father, and Savior. In the center, rested a gate of bronze with the letters "I AM" written across them. The inscribed words were in every tongue, and I somehow understood them all.

The legion of angels followed me and waited. I enjoyed being their leader. Rather than pulling the gate open, I floated through the entrance. I expected to be the only one — the first to enter—but found myself sandwiched among the billions. I didn't like being so close to them.

Who are these angels? Why did they arrive before me?

"This is beyond amazing," the angel with golden feathers said. I thought his breastplate and pants appeared dark due to the poor glow of the Fog, but in the light, they remained a dark gray color. The contrast made the gold outline stand out, despite our dazzling surroundings.

I wanted to disagree with the angel, but the splendor of the glowing palace could not be ignored. Rubies, emeralds, topaz, onyx, sapphires, and every beautiful stone imaginable came together to form an array of glory. The gold path divided among twelve ivory gates, each inscribed with a different name.

Within the palace, angels clothed to match and identical in physical features guarded the twelve gates. One pair of wings lifted the angels slightly above the golden street. Another pair of wings covered their face, and yet another pair concealed their feet.

From the archway marked "Judah," a Celestial Being approached. Long white robes hid his hands and feet, and a blue sash ran diagonally from his right shoulder to left hip. If he had wings, I didn't see them.

"Welcome," the Being said. "Come with me; I will show you my tabernacle."

My tabernacle? That seems possessive.

The Being looked directly at me like He could see into my mind. I felt apprehensive and pretended to ignore His peaceful hazel eyes, black shoulder-length hair and trimmed beard. Somehow, I found the Being to be annoying and engaging. I wanted to ask His name, but assumed He didn't know it.

I followed the Being. His long robes trailed behind him, keeping me further away than I wanted. We flew to a courtyard about 150 feet long and seventy-five feet wide and high. Sturdy red-wood pillars supported the frame made of four layers of cloth. A veil hung between five golden pedestals.

The Being pointed to the curtain, and the veil parted in two from top to bottom, allowing us to enter.

The angel with golden feathers and several around him gasped.

My mouth fell open in awe.

I stood on white marble with a golden lamp-stand on my left and a table on my right. Fire bloomed from the six branches of the lamp-stand.

"The Light of the world," the annoying tour guide said, "and the Bread of life." He gestured to the table overlaid with gold, three feet long and one foot tall. Golden plates, bowls, and jars held twelve loaves of fresh baked bread, filling the air with a rich yeast aroma.

In the middle, smoke rose from the altar of incense. At seven feet wide and long, the altar appeared large within the cramped room. The feeling came from the million other angels surrounding me, making my breathing increase. I wanted to break free from the confining area. My uneasiness became overshadowed by the sweetness of frankincense and myrrh mixed with the bread, giving the room a pleasant ambiance.

In front of another veil, stood an angel. Silver chain-mail peeked from under long white robes, tied with a gold sash around his waist. Locks of straight blond refused to hide from beneath a white hood. Stainless steel and light blue stones sheathed a broadsword.

What is the armor for? Where did he get the weaponry?

The suited angel knelt to his knee in front of our guide. It seemed a little dramatic, not to mention backward. We were unarmed and yet the defended one submitted.

"Stand, Gabriel," the white-robed Celestial Being said.

The armored angel stood. He had a name! Where did he get such a thing? I wanted one!

Gabriel lifted a pitcher from the table and poured clear water into a large bronze basin. "Come, be cleansed."

One angel after another washed their hands. I watched thousands of "cleansings," expecting the water to darken, but the liquid never changed. After circling the cramped room, Gabriel offered the basin to me.

"No," I said.

"All who enter must be cleansed," Gabriel said.

"I am," I said. "The water has remained pure. There's no need for this ritual."

"Allow me," the tour guide said.

"No, my Lord." Gabriel lowered his head to the Being.

"For no one comes to the Father, except through me." The guide dipped His hands into the basin and washed them. The water covering Him turned to dark red, pouring from His wrists.

What is this magic?

Gabriel remained still as the rest of us fluttered back.

"What is that?" I asked. "Why did it turn red?"

"It's my blood." answered our guide.

When the Being removed His hands from the basin, they were clean. Not a drop of blood stained His cloak. He took the basin from Gabriel, whose arms remained the same as if the bowl had not been moved. The Being carried the blood and poured the vital fluid over the altar. Dark-red liquid ran over the bronze.

I should have simply washed like the others. Why did I feel the need to be different?

"It has been paid," our guide said.

"What's been paid?" I asked.

"Man's debt."

I wanted to question Him further but fell silent as He approached the second veil.

Threads of blue, purple and scarlet were woven together. The curtain looked impossible for one angel to move, but I had learned to stop underestimating our guide. Whatever He was, He wasn't like the rest of us.

The veil separated, beams of light broke through. The glow was brighter than the first created light. I stood before the source of all. Everything that came and was to come would originate right here.

From every direction, voices sang. "Alleluia, Alleluia, Alleluia... For the Lord, God-Almighty reigns... Holy, holy, holy..." The songs blended in perfect harmony. I wanted to join them, but feared my cry would not match their perfection.

"Come forth," echoed a voice from above the light. At the sound of His calling, my knees gave way, and my body fell prostrate. My breaths came in pants, and my wings fluttered wildly, yet I remained in place.

Only our guide stood. He lifted His robes to place a scarred foot on a crystal step. As He ascended, the multitude cheered.

I needed to know more about this Being. What injured such a powerful Guardian? While trembling, I placed my foot on the clear staircase. With each step of faith, I followed my guide. I felt the presence of the other angels I had led joining me.

The singing multitude continued, their backs to the light. Behind them, others played the trumpet, lyre, flute, and harp. Their eyes remained closed as they swayed in worship.

At the top of the staircase, the Being walked across the surface, yet His feet didn't touch the ground. He didn't need wings because the translucent Fog carried him.

"Arise. The place where on thou stand is holy ground," the blinding Light said.

With a flap of my wings, I hovered over the surface. The Being rode the Cloud to the throne. Seven torches lined the path. I imagined the amount of diamonds it would take to reflect light from every angle. In true brilliance, every color of the rainbow sparkled back at me.

From their seats came flashes of lightning followed by rolling thunder. Their thrones floated on a lake of clear crystal.

To my astonishment, our tour guide took a seat to the right of the Light. Who shone so brightly I could not see his face if I tried. Fear kept me from looking. Angels fell before the two seated on Their thrones and worshipped Them as One.

"All hail the Trinity," chanted the angels.

"What is the Trinity?" the shirtless angel asked.

"You mean Who?" Corrected Gabriel. "The Trinity is God, three equal parts but One whole."

"Worthy are You, our Lord and God, to receive glory and honor and power. For You created all things, and by Your will, they existed and were created."

Then the Cloud transformed into a small white flying creature with tiny feet and a beak. Its feathers appeared soft and gentle. The animal perched on the shoulder of the Being seated next to the shining Light.

"Who are you?" I mumbled.

"I AM" the Guardian said. With those simple words, I knew He wasn't simply a Being. He was God, who humbled himself by taking a visible form. "I am Jehovah," our guide said.

"Come, my angels," the blinding Light said.

My brain could not process such humility. I didn't understand why, but I felt the urge to try to be like Him.

"Go ahead." I gestured to those behind me, waving them forward. The one with golden feathers followed my example and did the same until we reached the end of the line.

Four creatures flew above the thrones. They had eyes along their front and back. The first had a large head surrounded by a full tan shaggy mane and razor-sharp teeth; the second's head was the same size as the first, but its short hair was muddled with black and brown. It also had pointed horns on either side. The third had the face of an angel, and the fourth had a narrow head and beak with feathers covering itself.

Each creature had six wings and never ceased speaking. "Holy, holy, holy, is the Lord God Almighty, who was, is, and is to come!"

They sang the same song as the other angels.

The last member of my legion approached the Trinity first. Metal wings sprouted from each shoulder and arched on either side, gathering above his short, mahogany hair, matching the bronze gauntlets over his forearms. A royal blue tunic could be seen under his breastplate.

"Your servant is here." He bowed before the throne.

"Rise, Cassiel," the shining Light said. "I bless you with My speed and this sword."

The small feathered creature used its talons to pick up the long saber, dripping with lightning. Sparks glowed from the tip, and the Spirit gave the weapon to Cassiel.

"Thank you, my Lord." He took the sword and gave another bow to Jehovah before leaving the Holy of Holies.

I waited and watched as each angel passed before the throne, receiving a weapon and their name.

"Rise, Nakir. Rise, Maalik. Rise, Sammael. Rise, Phanuel."

Phanuel was the shirtless one who warned me about touching the planet's rings. He wore only a white kilt and received no equipment with which to defend himself. I didn't understand the purpose of the weapons but, more than that, I wondered why Phanuel was given nothing.

"Did you hear?" I asked the one with golden feathers. "To be called, 'the face of God', what must that be like?"

"I do not know. It almost makes up for the lack of defense. I am beginning to feel anxious to receive mine."

"Your name or your weapon?" I asked.

"Both," he answered.

My patience wore thin as hundreds of thousands of angels approached the throne. Finally, only my friend and I remained.

"After you," the one with golden feathers said.

I stepped forward, then stopped. If I left now, would I be able to find him again within the multitude? Without knowing his name, I could lose the only angel I had grown to admire.

"Go, ahead. I'll wait," I said.

He bent his arm over his chest and bowed in respect to me. I smiled and nodded. The admiration felt wonderful. I had done the right thing in allowing those behind me to go first. My companion floated to the throne.

"Your servant is here," he said, dropping to his knees and stretching out his arms to Jehovah and his Maker.

"Rise, Michael. I have blessed you with discernment in all My ways," the Light said.

He received a round shield and short sword, both dark gray and edged in gold, like his wings and armor. The weapons appeared large in the thin talons of the gentle white fowl.

"Thank you, my Lord." Michael took the equipment. Over his shoulder, he looked to me. His lips formed a grin, but the pleasure didn't reach his eyes which remained serious.

"Well done," I mouthed, certain he would not be able to hear me above the chorus of voices.

Once Michael left the room, I flew toward the throne. The Trinity didn't need to tell me to come forth, I learned from those before me.

"I am here." I looked into the face of the Being who had given me the grand tour not mentioning He belonged in the High Places. With the fear subsiding, I tried to look at the other figure. I could not see due to the brightness.

"What shall I call you?" I asked the Light.

"I AM." The pillars shook at the sound of his voice. I found my knees tucked to my chest and my arms lifted over my head. My wings kept me from touching the holy ground. "I am Elohim."

My tongue felt heavy, preventing me from speaking.

"Rise!" Elohim said.

I obeyed His command and rose. The Spirit delivered a stainless-steel shield with a slithering thing across the front to me. The thin sword had jagged points along one side. I took the equipment from the creature's grasp. The metal felt cold and strong.

I turned to leave His presence when I realized I didn't know my name. Had he spoken the words, and I was so dumbstruck that I missed them? Possibly.

Part of me wanted to flee. But the day would come when Michael and the others I had led would ask. I needed to tell them my name.

I could make something up. Name myself. The idea had a strong appeal. No one would know.

I smiled, liking that decision.

Then a voice from above said, "Oh, Morning Star, son of the morning. You shall be called, Lucifer!"

CHAPTER TWO

He hath made the Earth by his power, He hath established the world by His wisdom, and hath stretched out the heavens by His discretion. When He uttereth His voice, there is a multitude of waters in the heavens, and He causeth the vapours to ascend from the ends of the earth; He maketh lightnings with rain, and bringeth forth the wind out of His treasures. - Jeremiah 10: 12-13 (KJV)

Lucifer? What kind of name was that? I wanted something that showed that Elohim had taken note of me and that I was special. It should be apparent that He saw part of Himself in me. God granted His strength to Gabriel; chose Michael to be like Him and in Phanuel He recognized His face by giving them names with those meaning. What did I get? Nothing!

"Lucifer," declared Elohim.

I turned to face His radiance.

"You are to select an apprentice."

"What should I teach him?" I asked.

"How to protect the holiness of God," answered Jehovah.

I nodded pretending to understand what He meant.

Pausing, I noticed the dazzling lights reflecting around me. I stood in the presence of The Light. Of course, His glow was bright!

But maybe, He wasn't the true source? I thought of myself in the same way Elohim had. Next to Him, I was brighter. Better.

I smiled. Yes, the name Lucifer served me well.

I gave the Trinity a final glance to see if they had anything further to say.

Neither looked at me.

Leaving the throne room, everything appeared darker, like a shadow hung over the palace. Maybe my light could brighten the walls of heaven? To test my ability, I drew closer to them, nothing changed.

"Why is the palace darker?" Gabriel asked.

I didn't have an answer, but since God gave me the position of teacher, I couldn't afford the appearance of ignorance. I avoided his question. Gabriel had a name before me and noticed changes to the palace I didn't.

"How long have you been here?"

"I came first, therefore He gave me the task of securing the entrance," answered Gabriel.

Clever. He didn't answer my question which made him appear as intelligent as me. "How many had gone before me?" I asked.

"Twelve million legions."

"Of course. Why is everything around here twelve?"

"I do not know." Gabriel's straight blond hair swooshed as his head shook. He wasn't as intelligent as I'd thought.

"You said the palace is darker. The gloom is not because I left up there, you know?" I nodded toward the throne room.

"No. Jehovah called the blackness 'night.' I didn't expect the darkness to affect the palace."

I thought about asking him why, but felt he didn't have an answer. Not to mention I'd reveal I was as clueless as him in the process. That would not be a good plan.

Filled with curiosity, I left in search of the darkness. Why create light for the glow to fail and become dark again? The cycle seemed broken to me and in need of further investigation.

I exited through the golden gate into the vastness of space. Light from the glowing palace landed on the watery planet. I wondered what became of the other eight planets the Fog had created. Would heaven's light reach that far?

I followed the glow until the light disappeared on the other side. Everything along the backside of the watery orb remained in darkness. My body relaxed and felt at peace. I came to the gloom to fix what I thought to be a problem of darkness. Instead, I enjoyed the shadow.

The light of Heaven no longer pierced my eyes. Despite there being no need to hide, I could within the blackness. I gazed into the eclipse, surprised to find something moving further below. I wasn't the only one who ventured here.

The angel's black armor and sword blended in perfectly, and he would've gone unnoticed had it not been for the white layer of feathers under his wings. I approached the angel.

"Who are you?" I asked.

"I am Abaddon." His eyes narrowed, and his mouth drew into a frown.

His demeanor made chills slither down my spine, making me feel apprehensive of him. I wanted to leave, but my curiosity got the better of me.

"What do you do here?" I asked.

His spiked hair swayed as he hovered in place. I waited so long for his answer; I almost forgot my question.

"Enjoy the solitude." He eyed me; clearly, I interrupted his version of tranquility.

"Sorry," I mumbled.

I fluttered past him, deeper into the darkness. I tried to understand why someone would not enjoy being included in the celestial palace. Heaven was far greater than I could imagine. I understood not wanting to spend time with the Master Tour Guide, but Elohim demanded praise.

No, He didn't. The worship He received was given willfully. As the great Master and Creator, He deserved all the accolades throughout the heavenly realm.

An odd smell caught my attention. The odor reminded me of the fire from the candles in the golden lampstand. As I moved further into the blackness, I saw puffs of gray. The smoke burned my nose. I brought my wings forward to blow the sulfur away.

"What's this?" I whispered.

My eyes widened to catch as much glow as possible to better see. I'm supposed to be the light-bearer. What happened to my glorious ability?

"Zophos," a deep sound answered.

I jumped and scanned for the voice, bringing my shield up to guard my face. I didn't understand the purpose of the armor but guessed Elohim gave us tools for a reason.

The mist tumbled together until the smoke rested against the dark robes of an angel. The material covered his eyes and body revealing only his lips and chin. His wings appeared black and smooth as if made from one large piece of flesh, not feathers like most other appendages.

He struck the tip of his halberd against the smoke and red sparks flew. From the ember's glow, I saw dozens of others like this one, surrounded by night.

"I am Maalik," the angel said. "You are the bright one."

"How do you know?" I asked.

"You are the only one who could reside in Elohim's presence and be considered beautiful," Maalik said.

"Uh... thanks?" I frowned and stepped back from him.

He stirred the odorous vapor with his feet, bringing flames to life. The fire singed his hair. I had been mistaken, he wasn't cloaked with a robe, but black locks which grew rapidly and ran down disappearing into the surroundings only to be licked by a scorching tongue.

"What's Zophos, and why are you here?" I asked.

"Jehovah sent me."

I scowled.

"He thought you would do that," Maalik said, his lips turning into a smirk. I wanted to see the rest of his face to know if he laughed at Him or me.

"Of course, He did. He thinks He knows *everything*. Sitting on a ridiculous throne does not make Him special."

"Indeed, it does," Maalik said. "But the throne does not make him powerful. He has that because of *who* He is."

I shook my head and sighed. "What are you doing here?"

"Waiting for you," answered Maalik.

"I had no plans to come here," I said.

"And yet," he stirred the smoke causing the sulfurous fog to billow into my face, "here you are."

I stared at his stern expression, wishing I could think of an intelligent rebuttal. Being a Creator didn't give Him the ability to foresee the future. Or, did it? An angry growl escaped from my chest as I had nothing to say.

I turned my focus away from Maalik and on those working around him. They gathered the smoke into sturdy columns and arranged the fog into archways and tunnels. For what purpose? One flap of my wings and their creation would disappear. Their hard work seemed futile, but Jehovah gave them a task. They began to work, and I explored new territory rather than find my pupil.

"Is there something I'm supposed to do?" I asked.

"Yes."

"What's my job?" I leaned closer to him. The fact the instructions didn't come directly from Jehovah bothered me greatly, but I would not have taken His words seriously. I hated He knew that.

"Observe," Maalik said.

I frowned. I hoped for something better and not to be a spectator. Maybe I should leave and begin the task Elohim gave me.

I stepped back, but his movements brought me back. He stirred the smoke with his long halberd. The fog swirled and grew wider. From within the vapor lifted a mirage of men without wings. They wore long red robes that swayed as they danced and sang praises to something other than God. They bowed to objects I had never seen before. I didn't understand but found the whole scene curiously exciting.

Suddenly, the people clutched their chest and fell. I watched them plummet further down until they rested in a puff of smoke. There, they cried out, and I heard the wailing and gnashing of teeth.

"Make the vision stop!" I yelled.

"What you see is not mine to control," replied Maalik.

"Then I will!" I flapped my wings wide and back again to displace the smoke, but the images didn't move.

The vision continued as the blood bubbled under their skin. Their flesh melted away until only bones remained. The anguished forms kept their eyes, which flowed with tears. Each drop sizzled as the sad moisture landed in the darkness. One after another, they experienced the same dreadful fate.

Like a warrior ready for battle, I screamed and brandished my sword. With all my strength, I plunged the weapon into the depth of the vapors. The skeleton split in half, bones scattering. Their cries surged as they spread out and echoed softly into silence.

I drove the sword into one victim after another, until they had all been dismembered. I destroyed them.

After lowering my sword, I took a deep breath and searched for Maalik and the others. Surely, they'd be impressed that I had overtaken the vision.

They were gone.

I glared. How did I not notice them abandoning their position? Next time, I'd make them stay.

Another puff of smoke captured my attention. Something had displaced the calm fog, revealing his location. Whoever had been there witnessed my accomplishment and would certainly tell the others. I wanted to know the name of my admirer, but the identity of the angel didn't matter. I knew he existed.

I left the darkness to return to the planet. Water crashed over the surface in rolling waves. I heard them splash. Their rhythmic movement gave me peace. While I enjoyed being near, I felt myself be pulled closer than I wanted to be.

Gravity grabbed me, pulling me into the light. A glow shone across the sphere. I could fly against the motion pulling me to Earth or relax and allow the force to move me freely.

Elohim said, "Let there be a vault between the waters to separate water from water."

One of the waves shot up, producing a geyser. The smell of crisp, clean air pleased my senses. Jets of water vaulted up into the sky resting in a new atmosphere. I smiled, looking at the gap between the layers of moisture. Unless the growing hemisphere were for me, I didn't understand why the Creator would do such a thing. The expanse seemed like a complete waste of space unless the area had a use. To the right and left, angels with the wind at their back kept the force from the

Earth. Before and behind me, heavenly warriors kept the blast at bay.

Clearly, He needed help. He brought me here for this purpose and not some ridiculous vision encased in smoke. Nature would become my student and obey my commands.

"Let's find out what I'm capable of," I mumbled.

I floated closer to the watery surface and dipped my toes into the cold wetness. Small ripples grew. I changed something God had made. Kicking through the water generated a large splash spraying around me. Encouraged, I spun through the liquid displacing everything around me. But the water settled back into place. I wasn't creating anything new. I tried again but had the same results.

What else did I have to work with?

After bringing my sword and shield to my chest, I dove through the water. I felt the gust trying to force me back out, which only made me fly harder. I needed to help Jehovah and to do something amazing.

I tasted the bitter, salty water. I didn't like the lasting residue in my mouth. The deeper I flew through the ocean, the darker my surroundings became. There were limits to the light's reach. That had to be a flaw.

If I had made the light, I would've given the brilliant glow the ability to pierce through anything. Maybe God had gifted me with an eye that saw what would make it better. My light would have the ability to pierce through the darkness. My pupils would learn easily and quickly. My power would grow and become greater.

I swam to the side and noticed something reflect back at me. I paused, and within the murky water, light showed. The new glimmer came directly from me. I had made something spectacular! Just as my name said, I had brought the light.

Well, well. So it seems I am Lucifer.

CHAPTER THREE

When he prepared the heavens, I was there. When He set a compass upon the face of the depth. When He established the clouds above. When He strengthened the fountains of the deep. When He gave to the sea his decree, that the waters should not pass His commandment: When He appointed the foundations of the earth.
- Proverbs 8:27-29 (KJV)

Submerged in the ocean, I watched the light expand. I was more powerful than I realized. The glow came closer, blinding me and burning until I turned my head.

Water gushed from the depths, tumbling me to the surface. I expected to be spit from the ocean, and out into space. Instead, I floated above the seas. The waves merged into a funnel that swirled and grew as the channel sucked in the tide. A cyclone twirled past me into another doubling in size. The waters parted, revealing, dry brown soil and two large scarred hands.

"Seas," Jehovah said and proceeded to tell the oceans how far to come to no longer cover the earth, speaking like a teacher and the liquid his pupil.

I thought I was to instruct the Earth. Why is He doing my task?

He gathered soil to form rolling hills and steep peaks. Sometimes, He sliced through them to create grand canyons and smaller valleys that rocks rolled down, settling on ledges or in ravines below. God tapped a large boulder with the base of His hand and water sprung forth. The liquid fell in great sheets, splashing into a pool below. With the tip of His finger, He carefully brought the water through the land to make rivers, streams, and lakes of various sizes.

Jehovah grinned His shoulders back with pride at His creation.

"Show off," I mumbled and flew higher to examine the sphere. My wet tunic kept me from breaking through the atmosphere as quickly as I wanted.

The planet remained mostly water, with one large land mass. Jehovah stood, looking at his creation as though he pondered what to do next. The pause made me want to leave, but I had the feeling I should stay.

"Let the earth bring forth grass." With a wave of His hand, sprouts of green emerged from the soil.

I darted to the surface to see tiny emerald blades run over hills and mountains. They snuggled close to rocks and other sediments. Once planted, their roots formed and the foliage remained in place.

Aromas rose I had never imagined possible. Freshly-tilled soil and new plants bloomed in all direction. Perfume erupted as large trunks erupted from the ground. The trees sprouted branches with leaves and colorful, sweet-smelling fruit. Thousands of variations mingled together and yet reproduced after their own kind.

The land blossomed at random except for one area. I watched Jehovah take great care in the formation of a garden. It rested in the east, and there God made all kinds of trees, each pleasing to the eye. I stood within the nursery and smelled the round apples, bright oranges, thick-shelled pomegranates, bananas and more fruits than ever before.

I wanted to take one piece from each tree to savor the uniqueness of God's creation, but everything happened so fast that if I blinked, I would miss something spectacular.

In the middle of the garden, two trees stood apart from the others. The first tree's leaves started green, turned to red and yellow before withering to brown. They broke from the tree and fell to the earth.

"What's this?" I asked.

"The Tree of Life," Jehovah answered.

"The tree is defective." I picked up a brittle leaf and crushed the foliage into smaller pieces. With a puff of my breath, the flakes left my palm and drifted helplessly in the wind.

"Wait."

I sighed and looked at the other tree which had fruits of various size and shapes together on the one branch. The tree also appeared to be deformed, since all other vegetation kept to their kind.

I wondered if Elohim would scold Jehovah for his mistake. I smirked at the thought. If He heard my thoughts, He didn't respond.

Out of the corner of my eye, I saw something change on the first tree. The Tree of Life sprouted purple flowers along the branches. I stood in awe as the petals grew and then also fluttered to the ground. In their place, new green leaves formed. A breeze filtered through the branches, causing them to wave. I remained transfixed by the amazing sight as I watched rotations of beauty.

I didn't like admitting that Jehovah was a powerful creator. As I retreated, He brought in a river to water the garden, which separated into four winding streams. I finished watching him. I felt awestruck at all He could do, but I didn't like the awareness. The excitement troubled me.

Other angels didn't appear to struggle in the same way I struggled. Or maybe, they did and didn't have anyone to share their feelings with. Considering that I had not shared my thoughts, most likely there were others. I needed to investigate. Hopefully, within them I would discover the apprentice Elohim asked that I find.

I flew up to the palace and entered through the golden gate. A chorus of angels greeted me, singing praises to God. One of them drew nearer to me and sniffed the air. I wondered if I smelled like Earth.

Their voices echoed throughout the palace, or perhaps, from every corner of heaven, everyone constantly gave adoration to their Creator. Their obsession with God was too great for me to process. I followed the murmur of voices to the grand banquet hall.

White marble lined a golden path and intricate archways. I recognized the craftsmanship to be vines and floral blooms interwoven. Light burst from the pillars, making the area easy to see and causing the many gems encrusted in the ceiling to glisten. The solid granite table stretched for miles in both directions. As far as I could see, angels took fruit from brass bowls and ate.

Michael stood amongst the crowd, speaking to an angel with wings so thin they appeared translucent. Over a white tunic, he wore a blue robe with bells and pomegranates evenly spaced along the bottom. A golden breastplate with twelve gems and names written across each jewel guarded his chest. Two additional stones sat on his shoulders. Blue, purple, and scarlet yarn wove together to create his turban and sash. A coat of the same colors in a checkered pattern completed his ensemble. It seemed a bit much. Maybe he didn't have a choice in what he wore. I certainly didn't select a one-shouldered tunic and sash to clothe myself in.

"Friend!" Michael said, grabbing a strawberry and waving to me. "Come, join us."

"Welcome. My name is Barachiel," the colorful one said.

"Nice to meet you." I hovered between them. We had no physical need for food, but the items had a rich aroma and pleasant taste. The camaraderie of feasting together felt nice. Between bites of food, they mumbled their thanks and admiration to Elohim.

There was no purpose or goal other than glorifying God. I felt appreciation toward my Maker, but I also longed for something more. Something I could call my own.

Michael bumped my shoulder. "What did He name you?"

Without a second of hesitation, I replied. "Call me Luc."

"Luc?" Barachiel repeated. "I do suppose you bring light and beauty with you." He smiled and seemed to be genuinely caring. The attributes made him weak.

Michael nodded and ate another strawberry. He said nothing about my apparent beauty and the absence bothered me. Did I not appear glorious to him? I could not see my wings well, but I felt their grandeur. They must have been larger than his golden-lined features.

"Have you seen the changes to Earth?" Michael asked.

"I have not," Barachiel said. "But I understand that is where this comes from." He gestured to the plentiful bowls before us.

"I was there," I said. "The waters parted and the first sprouts formed."

A hush fell over the banquet as I elaborated on the scene displayed in front of me. The creation of vegetation had been spectacular to see firsthand, but I made the formation seem more awe-inspiring as I described the foliage coming to life.

"I created a…"

"You did?" Michael broke through my explanation.

"What?" I asked, irritated by the interruption from my friend. I became so involved in the recreation of the experience that I had put myself in the place of Jehovah. The exaggeration was accidental, but now I didn't know what to do. I could not backtrack because then I would be seen as weak, which I was not.

"The trees were magnificent. One had an assortment of fruits while the other mesmerized me with its continual changes. Both are awe-inspiring." I continued with the description of the garden, hoping they'd forget my moment of embellishment.

Soaking in my words, I recognized many who had followed me on the first day. Once again, I became their leader, the one they admired. I had completed Elohim's task without having to try. Superiority came naturally to me.

Phanuel's countenance glowed like a young angel who heard something special for the first time. I liked that I could entertain his imagination. Seeing his enthusiasm made me wish I had someone to do the same for me. I wanted to dream big and believe anything was possible. Then, I could be like God.

With that simple thought, the brass bowl shook against the granite table. A platter toppled off the edge of the table spilling apples. They rolled along the marble floor as the room continued to tremble.

Michael's hand reached for his sword as his other arm lifted his shield.

"What's happening?" Phanuel asked. The angel had no defense other than his strong arms and back. He seemed youthful with his body appearing physically fit and ready for battle. The perfect contrast within an innocent warrior.

I stood in front of Phanuel willing to protect him from the quivering room.

"Thank you," he said.

His words confirmed the gratitude and loyalty I felt within him. Being able to sense his emotions was an additional skill I didn't know I had. Maybe, I had learned something new. I wanted more new abilities. Who else could I bring under my wing? To mentor and provide for them. Would I hear their voice inside my head like I did with Phanuel?

The translucent Fog entered the banquet hall through the jeweled ceiling. The cloud swirled along the outer perimeter, capturing the attention of all.

I didn't know what to make of the Godly-Spirit. Was the Fog to be worshiped the same as Elohim and Jehovah?

Those around me fell silent. The Mist flew down and hovered above my head like a halo. My long blond hair swirled into my face and I raised a hand to settle the strands. I had been selected for something, but I didn't realize what.

Did the Spirit perceive my desire to better myself and to lead others to their full potential as a threat? If God was all-knowing, then He must know my true intentions. Nothing would surprise Him.

"This angel speaks untruthfully," someone said. I had not noticed him before, but immediately thought I should have. Similar to Phanuel, he wore strips of torn cloth around one arm, covering half his breast and his neck, leaving most of his torso and arms bare. His feathers reached down to his feet and crowned above his head in four talon-like fingers. Coiled on his hip hung a whip with lightning and fire sparking from the tip.

"I did not!" I glared at the stranger. "Who are you?"

"I'm Sammael, and I was with Elohim when Jehovah did what you have claimed."

A chill slithered down my spine and boiled within my gut at the same time. How dare he!

The Fog circled me. Did I make claims meant only for Jehovah? I didn't mean to do anything wrong! I had created light within the depths of the waters. The accomplishment seemed impressive at the time, but immediately paled in comparison to the Creator.

From within the Mist, a voice called me to the throne room. Looking around, I felt certain no one else heard the words.

I'm coming; I told God.

The Holy Spirit ascended through the jeweled ceiling, I assumed back to Jehovah and Elohim inside the throne room.

"If you'll excuse me," I said to Michael and those gathered in the banquet hall. I stepped to the door, and so did many others. They blocked my path, forcing me to wait.

"I must go, as well," Phanuel said.

"Where to?" Barachiel asked, and I wondered the same.

"To the throne room," Michael, Phanuel, and I said in unison. We glanced at each other with our eyebrows scrunched.

"He called you, too?" I asked.

"Yes," Sammael answered.

"Great," I mumbled.

Was nothing sacred around here? I didn't need an audience while being scolded. I felt confident He would give me a warning and, in return, I'd agree never to embellish the truth again. We'd have a quick and simple conversation.

There was no need for the whole legion to be involved. To my dismay, the entire herd followed me. Moments before, I had wanted to be their leader, but now I'd rather be left alone.

What would God do to me? Throw me out into the void of space like he had the other planets? I hoped not. My wings twitched in anticipation as did those around me. Is that what they wanted to see? Me being banished?

Looking into their faces, nothing resembled resentment nor a desire for ill will toward me. But what would those expressions look like? In need of a description, I thought of Abaddon. He had sought out the darkness and found solitude there; the same way as I had. The eeriness of him and Maalik perplexed me but, in their presence, I didn't feel they wanted harm to come to me.

I didn't understand our purpose here, but I had more to offer than simply singing praises to my Creator. I wanted God to see my true potential and, if He already did, to reveal that fullness to me.

With renewed energy, I flew down the long corridor, leaving my legion of followers trailing behind.

Placing one foot in front of the other, I arrived at the base of the crystal staircase. I remembered following Jehovah and trusted the clear path to carry me closer to Elohim. This time, I didn't have to rely only on faith; I had been there and saw the way with my eyes.

A battle waged within me. I wanted to apologize for my mistake, but also didn't like admitting to the blunder. Oddly enough, God had given me the ability to err. I wondered what else I could do. Now was not the time to dream of possibilities.

I needed to make things right with Jehovah and Elohim. As I ascended the staircase, millions from the banquet hall followed me. Why did God allow them to come? Should not my admonishment be private?

Again, I remembered the humility of Jehovah and the desire to be like Him. That devotion led me to allow those behind me to go first. In this case, I should be a shining example for my comrades. I'd show them how to repent justly and to remain in Elohim's good grace, furthering my assignment to be their teacher.

I wished my breathing would settle. Instead, my gasps came and exited in rapid succession. Did my reaction make me appear scared? I could not allow that to happen. I squared my shoulders and marched to the light.

The angelic songs I heard last time were a faint echo. Only the harp and flute remained in the Holy of Holies along with the four flying creatures.

"Lucifer, come forth," Elohim said.

I walked between the glowing torches and took the final steps required to be directly in front of Jehovah, who sat next to the Bright One and the Fog's fowl form perched on Jehovah's shoulder. Lightning and thunder continued to battle within the crystal sea at the base of their thrones.

"Remove your weapons," Jehovah said. He gestured to the clear pit.

I didn't want to lose my weapons. I remembered the vision and how I had scattered it into pieces. For a second, the thought of defying Him drifted across my mind. I shook my head, destroying the notion. I'd be a good example for others to follow.

I laid down my shield. It floated in place over the translucent sea. Hoping my sword would do the same, I sat it on top of my shield. I had not realized how emotionally dependent on the armor I had become. Without my equipment, I felt naked and exposed. Regardless, I lowered to one knee before the Trinity, keeping my face to the ground.

"Do you not know there is nothing hidden from His sight?" Jehovah asked. "For all things are open and laid bare to the eyes of Him."

Let us teach you. I heard in my mind from the Fog.

"I accept," I whispered, unsure if Jehovah and Elohim heard me the same as the Spirit.

Jehovah rose from the throne. As he came down the staircase, he lifted the hem of his white robe, revealing scarred feet. What could harm him in such a way to mark his body? Did that make him weaker than the Spirit or Elohim?

I felt His gaze before seeing the confirmation that Jehovah indeed did look to me. In His eyes, I saw compassion, mercy, understanding, and love.

After He passed by, I stood at an angle to see Them. The mist hovered within the vacated throne as Elohim remained in place. I wondered about His features and if He would allow me to see His face or any physical part of His form. Maybe, that was Jehovah's role, to be the hands and feet of God.

"Nothing that has come or is yet to come is by accident," Jehovah said.

"Are you sure?" I moved closer to my weapons, keeping watch over them. The shield continued to carry the sword as they drifted along the crystal sea.

"Yes," Elohim answered.

"For I am here because of a mistake," I reminded Him.

"Yours, not mine," replied Jehovah.

"And the marks on you. They were done on purpose?"

"Yes and no."

The tip of my toe grazed the ground, and I felt the surface tremble. Immediately, I flapped my wings to keep my full foot from pressing against the floor. I remembered Elohim instructing us that the ground was holy and not to be touched. I felt Jehovah's gaze as he watched me.

He continued. "I will allow them to happen."

"Will? It hasn't happened yet?"

"No," Jehovah answered.

"How?" I asked. Why did He have to be so mysterious?

"You will see. One day."

With each encounter with Him, I found myself filled with more questions than receiving answers.

Sammael approached us, his whip lying helplessly in his palms outstretched in submission. "My Lord, what is to become of Lucifer?"

"What do you think should happen?" Jehovah asked.

"Judgment. There must be consequences," replied Sammael.

"There will be."

My chest rumbled as I turned to face my accuser. "The words that came from my mouth were unintentional." Then my focus turned to God. "You know me."

"That I do," Jehovah acknowledged.

"Sammael doesn't understand because he wasn't there. I was there. You allowed me to see something amazing and, when explaining the creation to the others, I misspoke. If you really know *all*, then I shouldn't be held responsible for magnifying the events."

"You claimed to do what I had done," Jehovah countered.

"For that, I am sorry." I lowered my head in resignation. "I know you wouldn't have done so."

"Nor could I," Jehovah said.

My head snapped up, looking at Him. Excuse me? Did Jehovah say there was something He could not do?

An awful note from the harp rang out as the angel stuck the wrong string, most likely astonished from what they heard from the powerful Creator. A mistake. We were capable of error. Something the Holy Trinity could not do.

I wondered what else was beyond their ability. Looking out at the great crowd of witnesses, I would have been embarrassed to admit a limitation, but God appeared peaceful. Of course, it was good *They* could not do wrong. Think of the calamity if they created something or someone they should not have.

Without intention, I had moved closer to Jehovah so we hovered near each other.

"Lucifer," Elohim said. His voice echoed through the expanse of heaven, and I felt a pause amongst the angels, all listening. "Let him who thinks he stands take heed lest he fall."

I nodded, but had no idea what he meant. "Of course," I said. Jehovah smiled which caused me to glare. "What?"

"He's saying do not be so arrogant. Even you are capable of falling flat on your face." Jehovah clarified.

"You'd love to see that," I said.

He shook His head. "I want no harm to come to you."

Elohim continued. "There hath no temptation overtaken you except such as in common: but *I am* faithful, who will not allow you to be tempted beyond what ye are able; but will with the temptation also make a way to escape, that ye may be able to bear it."

My eyes darted to Jehovah.

This time, the explanation came through the Holy Spirit speaking directly into my mind. *Remember God will never abandon you, nor let you be pushed beyond your limit. He will help you through any circumstance.*

"So, basically, if I mess up again, then it's actually Your fault? 'Cause, You should have gotten me out of the situation."

Jehovah shook his head, again. The colorful gems surrounding the throne room reflected across his face making a rainbow. "The method of escape is provided. Failure to take it, is on you."

"What if I do not see what you provide?" I asked.

"Then you weren't looking hard enough," Jehovah answered.

Easy for Them to say. What if it's like whispering something and then punishing the listener for not hearing? The Trinity's standard didn't sound fair. They wanted me to trust Them and Their words were meant to be comforting, but it was not.

"I came here to apologize, and I have already done so. Am I free to go?" I asked.

"We have chosen you for a special purpose and, for that reason, we offer to you grace," Elohim said. His voice came out of the thunder rumbling through the walls of heaven. "Do not think of yourself more highly than you ought. Consider this your only warning."

The eyes of my legion fell upon me. God revealed to everyone that I was the Chosen One, and that I would be given a task greater than any other.

He didn't say that, I heard from the Fog.

It could have been what He meant. Regardless, I needed to slow down. I didn't have to be the best in the world, but simply knowing Elohim had something in mind for me specifically made my chest swell with pride. How incredibly awesome!

A gust of wind tore through the light of Elohim, gathering the glow to form an arm. The surrounding legion and I gasped. Something more amazing than the creation of the planets, the oceans being directed into place, or the plants leaping on Earth was about to happen.

The great Light scooped up my sword and shield from the crystal sea. I had forgotten about them. They had become unimportant compared to the great quest God had in store for me.

Elohim remained on the throne, but his glow brought the weapons to me. They hovered in the air.

I glanced at Jehovah, uncertain on what to do.

"Take them," he said.

I reached into the Light, grabbing the shield's base, and again with my other arm, as my fingers wrapped around the glowing sword. From over my shoulder, Michael shielded his eyes from my radiance.

"My Son," Elohim said. "It's time to give light to the night."

CHAPTER FOUR

And I will make thy seed to multiply as the stars of heaven, and will give unto thy seed all these countries; and in thy seed shall all the nations of the earth be blessed.
- Genesis 26:4 (KJV)

The ground rumbled, and lightning shot from the jewel-encrusted ceiling of heaven. The rainbow of stones became clear, allowing us to look into the darkness of night. My mouth hung open at the oddity. Apparently, God wanted all to see the next stage of his creation.

From His glow, Elohim spoke, "Let there be lights in the firmament of the sky to divide the day from the night."

The fog swirled around Jehovah and together they made two lights, one greater than the other. The large one He commanded to rule over the day, and the lesser He gave dominion over the darkness.

Stepping back from the crystal sea, I bumped into Michael. His dark gray armor with gold trim glimmered in response to the new lights. Phanuel stood on my other side. His eyes remained transfixed by the night sky.

It wasn't how I would have done things. I wanted the better to be over the darkness because I found comfort in the shadow. But, as the larger one expanded I noticed its blaze took the place of heaven's and illuminated the Earth. Hot bubbling gas filled the sun and shared its warmth with the planet. The glow eliminated the darkness, while the smaller one complemented the night, reflecting the glow of the larger. These two lights worked in harmony with one another rendering the original source of light no longer necessary. It remained in the heavens.

I hated to admit the system worked well. The heavenly host applauded for the Creator of two round lights that rotated around the Earth. Then, with a wave of His hand, the planet tilted on its axis and spun for seasons, days, and years.

For what reason did God invent time? I saw no purpose in knowing how long we existed. Other than singing praises and fellowshipping in the banquet hall, they had no purpose. God promised me something special. Maybe, the task involved a specific time. These changes to Earth could be for me.

"Our God is amazing," whispered Michael.

"What do you think all this is for?" I asked.

"I do not know," replied Michael.

"Any guesses?" I asked.

"No, but Jehovah will not keep us wondering. He will supply us with answers."

"You seem confident. Maybe, the new creations are for you," I suggested to determine if his thought process was the same as mine.

Michael's eyes widened. "No, never."

"I have a different opinion of Him."

"Confusion is not bad," Phanuel said. "Sometimes I get the answer right, and other times the Spirit whispers another explanation."

Apparently, I wasn't the only one who drew incorrect conclusions. What purpose could mistakes have? Why were we given this ability?

A new feeling came which made me question myself. I no longer seemed as certain of what I should or should not do. What if my actions were wrong? Anxiety bubbled within me and then subsided as I thought of doing something God could not. Granted, the skill wasn't something good, but the addition left me wondering what other things could only I do.

My thoughts were interrupted as Jehovah took from the fog smaller glowing balls of gas. The mist rolled, changing them from green to yellow and then purple and red. The beauty transfixed me. Suddenly, He kicked the spheres and they exploded into colorful particles in the sky. The heavens broke out in cheers, and I felt the urge to join them.

One explosion followed another with each one more fantastic than the last. The stars shot out and then wove together to form a celestial being with a sword sheathed on his side.

"It is us!" exclaimed Gabriel.

I flew into the darkness and stood within the frame of stars. The constellation fits me perfectly. I loved seeing myself displayed amongst the sky.

Shouting for joy, I joined the heavenly host in giving glory to God.

We sang. "At your name, we will bow and the Earth will rejoice. The mountains shake, skies ring out in adoration. The oceans rumble and the trees wave at Your name…"

I once worried my voice would not blend well with the harmonies of the heavenly host, but now I found my sound complimented them well. Though we sang together, *my* voice filled the sky with endless acclamation. Jehovah had outdone himself. His powers amazed me.

The next batch of stars formed long lanes swirling to appear like a grand spiral staircase like those which led to the throne room.

Clever.

Murmurs of acknowledgment could be heard from within heaven. Being surrounded by stars, I enjoyed watching the show take place around. From within the firmament, a bright formation spread wide from a central location like wings. With each new star formed the universe, filling with colorful gas more spectacular than the next. It became clear there was no end to the Creator's ability.

In tribute to the chorus of voices and the skill of the musicians, more constellations formed in coordination to the beats of their song. The performance continued for hours not because Jehovah could not accomplish everything at once, but to allow us the pleasure of experiencing the magnitude of space.

I wanted to curse the sun as its light blocked the view of the stars from Earth. Why did He keep creating things for them to later be unseen? Was He so humble he'd make our applause come to an end?

If I were the Master, I'd never stop creating or distract the angelic hosts by something else. If I used my light to entertain, the show could continue. Bringing together gas and dust, I formed the stars into a pillar.

"Make another!" Phanuel said.

I smiled at my creation until the illumination erupted as a supernova collided into the column, sending smoke and rings of fire in all directions.

"Whoa," I said.

Immediately I created more with each one exploding. Now the angels watched me as I continued the show. With a grin, I gathered gas and brought chemicals behind it, creating a tail. The comet shot away from the sun.

I had created something! I loved doing new things and watching my powers grow. What else might I be capable of? The possibilities seemed endless.

Suddenly, I felt pulled into the comet's vortex. The force frightened me until I saw Jehovah riding along. Why did it have to be Him? He didn't have to ride on *my* comet.

Yes, the comet was mine! He'd probably claim He had created the falling star when the meteorite was all me.

"You should hold on," Jehovah said.

"What for?"

Instead of answering me, He spoke to the comet, telling the shooting star where to go. The comet was a lump of gas and filament brought into formation, not an intelligent being.

To my surprise, the comet shot out, going faster than I dreamed possible. In the time it took to blink, we passed by the eight other planets with moons and stars around them. In their glow, the spheres looked more spectacular than when first created.

The full expanse of space was greater than I could imagine. Galaxies with mesmerizing colors flashed past.

"What are you doing?" I asked.

"Showing you the fullness of my creation."

"What for?"

"To help you to understand my power," Jehovah said.

Fueled by some type of magic, the comet ducked and weaved through the starry formations. I wanted to abandon this crazy ship and slow down to enjoy the splendor. When the formations leaped before the heavens, it had been quite a show, and I wanted to go back to that excitement.

But I didn't want to leave Jehovah. I didn't enjoy His presence, but being here was an important step in my journey. Since leaving the Holy of Holies, I knew God had a purpose for me and I remained anxious to know the details.

"You wanted to know why I chose to show you the expanse of my creation," Jehovah said.

"Basically, you're gloating. That doesn't seem God-like."

The comet wove through a stream of galaxies. Lights as tiny as the tips of my fingers stitched together to form beautiful pictures in the sky.

"I am a jealous God," Jehovah said. "I do not want those inferior to think they are like me."

I narrowed my eyes at him. "I'm not inferior. Nor am I the one with scars along my body." I peered closer to his hand to get a better view of his permanent wounds. He had been pierced by something sharp and square. I saw many weapons, but nothing would leave such an indentation.

"I told you, I choose to bear these marks."

"But you didn't tell me why. Instead, you simply don't want me to be overly-confident."

"That is correct," Jehovah said and then whispered to the comet, directing its path.

"There are other angels like me. Or maybe, we are all this way. If that's the case, then why bring me alone on this journey?"

"Who says I haven't already shown the others?"

"You're evading my question." I ducked to avoid being struck by a star. "Come on, comet, pay attention to where you're going!"

"You speak to the falling star as well." Jehovah smirked, appearing the most playful I had seen Him, perplexing me.

"You have a clever tactic, but one easily seen through," I said. "Maybe you should stop being so transparent and say what you brought me out here to say."

"I have nothing further to offer."

"I doubt that. You pretend that you simply wanted me to see how far into space you've created. Is there an ending?"

"I am the beginning and the end."

"You are also annoying."

"Only to you."

"Is that so? It seems you have not met Abaddon. He does not enjoy the company of those in the palace." I grinned, feeling confident I had made a solid case for myself. The dark angel had been brooding to himself in the gloom. He took solitude in being away from the golden castle.

"Do you think he named himself?" Jehovah asked.

I looked at him, curious if he knew I considered doing that to myself. He had the ability to read my mind and peer into my spirit. Instead, He knew me so intimately that my thoughts and actions were no surprises to him.

"No," I answered. "I believe I am the only one who considered such a thing."

"Of that, you are correct."

I smiled, pleased to be selected from the others.

To some, my behavior might be seen as negative, but I saw my actions as someone who didn't let a silly thing like not knowing his name slow him down.

At some point, we must have circled the expanse of space because we arrived back at heaven. Or, the palace stretched across the breadth of the cosmos. Either option baffled me.

"Thanks for the tour. It's something you're great at."

Jehovah nodded. "Lucifer, you have much work to do."

I thought for a moment, but felt certain Jehovah had not given me a task. Once again, the temptation to pretend to know something grew.

In His great patience, Jehovah waited. I knew He wanted me to ask about my work, which was precisely why I didn't want the words to come.

You are foolish and stubborn, a voice in my head said.

I wasn't sure if the words came from the Spirit or Jehovah. Regardless of who said them, they spoke truthfully.

"It's time," He said.

Finally, I held back the question no longer. "Time for what? What is it you want me to do?"

"You are powerful, full of wisdom and talent. I am making you chief among the cherubim. You are being held responsible to protect the holiness of God. Now, build your army."

"Excuse me?" I asked.

CHAPTER FIVE

There stood a man over him with his sword drawn in hand: and Joshua went to him, and said unto him, "Art thou for us, or for our adversaries?" And he said, "Nay; but as captain of the host of the Lord am I now come."
- Joshua 5:13-14 (KJV)

Without another word, the Spirit swirled around Jehovah, lifting Him away. What did I need an army for? The Lord didn't say, but I thought of no one else better suited for the task than Michael. Instead of choosing him, Jehovah selected me, making me best among the cherubim.

I fluttered through the golden gate, entering the palace. I arrived at a location I had never been to before. I had grown accustomed to hearing the strum from a harp and the melody of the flute followed by the blast of the trumpet echoing throughout the halls of heaven. Today was similar except for the addition of a ting as metal struck against metal.

The syncopated clang didn't compliment the music but drew me in. Leaving the golden streets behind, I entered a wide-open space. Gray marble lined the floors and pillars supported the intricately-chiseled ceiling. Every weapon imaginable adorned the walls. The lowest level had shields, some so large the whole body could hide behind it. I had no need to rest and felt certain we could not tire, but the large mass would be cumbersome and difficult to manage.

The shields left me wondering, what we need guarding from? Was there an adversary God is preparing us for? With strong warriors as my army, I imagined the weaklings we would overpower. As I looked at the weaponry and angels nearby, I could determine the equipment that would serve them best. I assumed Elohim had the same skill when he administered our weapons.

Could we be injured or destroyed?

I thought of the scars on Jehovah's body and quickly decided the answer was yes. If He could be injured, then so could all of us. Also, having the armory would be pointless and this massive practice room completely worthless if the purpose wasn't to prepare us for battle.

From above the shields, I saw a dagger. The weapon rested in a brown case with straps to be tied to a person's thigh or calf. I placed my round shield on an empty peg and picked up the dagger. I removed the sheath. The curved blade glistened in the light peering through the crystal windows. My sword hung at my hip and I didn't feel the dagger would be needed at this time, but if something changed I'd return for it.

I set down the dagger and grabbed my shield before fluttering to the top where the broadswords hung. Beautiful jewels encrusted along the handle and the golden blades pointed down like grand crosses up in the sky.

Hundreds of pairs of warriors dueled against one another. Sparks shot out as metal ground against metal.

Gabriel, with his straight blond hair and smooth white robe, radiated a rainbow of colors along the length of his broadsword which he held with both hands.

Against him fought Cassiel. He had been first from my legion to receive his name. Tiny bolts of lightning charged his bardiche. His copper wings and armor reflected the light his weapon made.

"Do you come here often?" I asked them.

"Every day!" yelled Cassiel.

Gabriel swiped at Cassiel's head, who ducked and plunged his sparkling bardiche forward.

"And you?" I asked.

Gabriel dodged and struck again at Cassiel.

"Today is my first," Gabriel answered. The blond angel seemed so peaceful and meek. His forcefulness surprised me.

Out of the corner of my eye, I saw a broad ax swing through the air, striking against an angel. The tumbling warrior had two sets of wings, one arched over his shoulders and the other wrapped around him like an extra pair of arms. I saw no legs, but in their place billowed a green fog. He had no weapon but directed his mist to go where he wanted.

The attacking angel swung his large ax again at the strangely disfigured being. He dodged and then wrapped his green mist around the other angel bringing him to a halt. The large ax remained over the angel's head, his muscles permanently flexed, like a statue.

Is that what becomes of angels when we are destroyed?

"It's his gift," Cassiel said, answering a question I didn't ask.

"What is? And, whose?" I asked.

"Dumah's, it's his green fog," Gabriel said.

I looked again at the creepy angel. His face remained narrow, and his hands were so thin I saw the bones beneath his flesh. Long thin dreadlocks of white hairs waved in the strong gust of his wings.

Jehovah had brought me here to begin building an army. I didn't know the purpose, but I wanted this green thing on my side.

"Have either of you fought him?" I asked.

"Dumah arrived the first day, and I have not seen him again until today," said Cassiel.

"Why come here so often?" I asked. "What are you fighting for?"

"I enjoy it," answered Cassiel.

"We do not fight, for we are on the same side," Gabriel said.

"Say that to the one turned into stone," I mumbled. "Armor lines the walls on all sides. Do you only train with the weapon Elohim provided or do you use these others?"

"Only this." Gabriel lifted his sword. The weapon appeared to be the same one I saw him with before entering the throne room and assumed the sword to be from Elohim.

"I use them all." Cassiel grinned, his eyes alight with pride.

"Good for you. Do you have a favorite?" I asked.

"Yes." Cassiel caught an arrow heading directly toward me and then threw the projectile back in the direction it came from. "If you want to see, then you'll have to fight me."

"I'll take that into consideration," I said. How difficult could it be? I would destroy him the same way I had those in the vision while on Zophos.

I strolled throughout the room, looking at the weapons and armor to choose from. The double-headed lance had an appeal, and the long staff would have its advantage. I studied a belt which held sharp round blades to be thrown at their adversary and considered fiery arrows to pierce through any target.

When Elohim demanded I place my weapons in the crystal sea, I didn't want to lose them. The sword and shield were my only options. Seeing a room full of armor made me want to try new equipment. Other than to shatter the vision, I had not tested their ability. Maybe, the experience had been sufficient to know the sword felt good in my grasp and my shield provided safety.

The flutter of wings brought with it whispered thoughts of those close. Their words were muddled, but I felt certain of their curiosity about me. Did they find me to be beautiful the way Maalik and Barachiel did? If I became a statue, I felt confident the figure would stand out as the most radiant of them all.

63

What if I were damaged? If I wore scars on my body the way Jehovah did, that would not be acceptable. I wished for Phanuel to be an option for a first duel. I had felt his admiration and was confident Phanuel would rather see me win even at his own expense. Elohim found him to be so weak that he wasn't given anything at all.

The thought of Sammael passed over my mind. What I would not give to best my accuser. His ridiculous whip and long-feathered wings would not be able to withstand the light I'd bring. I imagined the beauty of his pathetic form being scattered by my sword.

Without realizing my actions, I circled the same simple dagger as before. I reached for the small weapon and wrapped the straps through my white garment to secure the case to my hip. My sword hung on the other side.

"Anything else?" Cassiel asked. He placed a helmet over his head, the metal nesting close to the brass wings on either shoulder. The additional armor made going for his head to be nearly impossible.

For a moment, I was tempted to add protection, but then shook my head.

"Do not lose," Cassiel said.

"Are there rules?" I asked.

Cassiel smirked. "I'll take it easy on you."

"That won't be necessary."

"I swear," Cassiel's voice echoed throughout the chamber, "we will end this duel standing."

"Very well. Shall we begin?" I drew my sword from its sheath.

"We shall." He held his long bardiche with both hands.

Circling him, drew the attention of the other dueling angels. This demonstration would make them want to be in my presence. I stood tall allowing my radiance to illuminate the area.

I floated in place as he scooted further from me

He was patient, allowing me to make the first move. Tension inched its way through my muscles.

In the space between us, I lifted my blade, and he blocked with the stem of his weapon. A second later, I heard the whoosh through the air as he sliced for my arm. I darted out of reach.

We tested our abilities and reflexes with similar moves but, Cassiel led the charge. The long staff of the bardiche took the force of my blade with ease. The clashing metal chimed out a melody as we danced back and forth, each blocking the other.

With a quick jab from Cassiel, a lock of my long blond hair fluttered to the ground. The severed tip darkened. I smelled the potent sizzle where the lightning within the bardiche had burned away my beautiful hair.

The crowd gasped.

An odor rose from the singed lock, reminding me of the sulfur surrounding Zophos. That had been too close. I had no intention of losing, but each time I saw a victorious move, I hesitated.

The admiration I felt toward Cassiel irritated me. I should be able to dispel him or encase his likeness in stone, whatever happened at the end of angelic duels, without the feeling of guilt.

"You're using *your* strength. Allow the weapon to lead," Cassiel instructed.

"Why should I take your advice? Your words might make it easier for you to win."

"It might. Or I could be an angel with noble intentions."

I didn't trust his advice. As I relaxed, the sword felt comfortable in my grasp like an extension of my arm. His advice helped but remained flawed. Did he know his words were wrong and tried to deceive me on purpose?

"There is no honor in a staged victory," I said.

"I would not be so sure."

With startling speed, he kicked against one of the grand pillars and shot directly at me. A chunk of marble fell from the structure and tumbled against the ground. I saw nothing below, for the night blocked the rays from filtering through the crystal glass. I remembered seeing the light reflect off the gem-encrusted weaponry and realized I had been in the practice room for longer than it felt.

Our audience grew as more gathered with the others to watch the display between Cassiel and myself.

With a strong flap of my wings, I flipped over Cassiel. Strips of my white garment fluttered behind my legs. My sword struck against the brass wing on his shoulder. The sound reverberated throughout the coliseum.

Dumah murmured, sounding like he was impressed by my movements.

"You're amazing," Cassiel whispered.

"And you thought you had to instruct me on how to fight." I chuckled.

"I was wrong."

"Could you say that a little louder? I almost missed it." I grinned which he returned. There was a camaraderie with

Cassiel that felt similar to Michael. He had been my first friend, and I wondered if he had been here to practice his skills. I imagined Michael as a natural warrior.

Cassiel swiped his bardiche at my feet, leaving a trail of sparks from the weapon's blade. As much as I admired him, it bothered me Elohim had given him such a spectacular weapon. I bore the light and therefore should have carried equipment that was my equal.

A strong desire to have what Cassiel had been given rose within me. I never felt anything like this impulse before. It filled me with renewed energy. If I could get the gleaming weapon from his hand and freeze him as Dumah had, then I'd claim the lightening bardiche for my own.

With added fervor, I fought against Cassiel. It took seconds for us to learn the other's preferences. His name meant god-like speed which he demonstrated with his incredible reflexes, but his eyes flinched from my radiance. I used my glow to my advantage and angled my body to intensify my light.

The whole room brightened as my glow reflected off the armor and weaponry around the room.

"It's beautiful," mumbled Cassiel.

"How many duels have you participated in?" I asked.

"Enough for Elohim to ask me to begin forming an army."

I frowned, having had Jehovah tell me to do the same. Had God made Their first mistake?

A rainbow of lights shown from within the heavenly palace. Distracted by the illumination, Cassiel didn't move as I dropped my shield and grabbed a crossbow from the mass of weaponry. I could not allow him to be given the same task as myself. Without hesitation, I squeezed the trigger.

A bolt shot out, landing perfectly through the side of his bronze armor. I knew destroying him would be easy the moment he challenged me to the duel. Today, I proved to myself and those watching I was the better warrior and leader.

Cassiel gasped and vanished, taking his lightning-infused weapon with him.

CHAPTER SIX

For we wrestle not against flesh and blood, but against powers, against the rulers of the darkness of this world, against spiritual wickedness in high places.
- Ephesians 6:12 (KJV)

The sound of my shield ricocheting off the ground below filled the hushed crowd. My breaths entered and exited rapidly as my fingers had a death grip on my sword. I lifted the weapon, ready for another challenge.

What had I done?

Angels around me had their mouth hanging open, and their eyes were wide with horror. Some had trained daily with Cassiel and knew his strength and power. I could become their teacher just as Elohim tasked for me and they would trust my leadership. My demonstrated skills earned the right for me to be called superior.

"Do not fear!" I commanded. "For Jehovah has selected me to form a great army. Allow me to become your master, and I will guide us to victory!"

I fluttered through the ranks of the hall, and as my light shone on them, courage would overtake many with insecurities. Others fled from the room. It had been a surprise to see my friend Cassiel vanish before our eyes. If I had known that would be the outcome, I might have hesitated. His demise would have come eventually, but I could've used his strength and skill to teach others.

Now, I was on my own.

"You!" I pointed to an angel with layers of golden and white garments "Shed your outerwear and take the weaponry I will select for you." While he disrobed, I flew to the highest heights and selected two bronze swords.

"I want to keep my staff," the golden angel said. I didn't bother asking his name because it didn't matter.

"Suit yourself." I tossed the two weapons to another and then gave them further instruction.

My attention returned to the angel with the staff. The remaining host of angels watched as the two beings dueled. I admired his use of the rod, but saw no way for him to overtake his adversary. Maybe Gabriel was right, and we were on the same side and therefore should be equal. The notion gave me pause.

I paired off others with shields and swords. A new song rang from the room as their weapons collided. Gabriel's two-handed sword slammed into his opponent's shield. The angel's arm shook, and his weapon slipped through his fingers.

"Get a new weapon," Gabriel instructed.

"Why not just destroy him?" I asked.

The defenseless angel trembled and bolted behind a pillar to protect himself. Hiding made him appear a coward.

"There is no honor in defeating a helpless being," answered Gabriel.

"Fair enough," I answered.

Out of the corner of my eye, Phanuel entered the wide space. I wondered what weapon he selected for himself. My view became blocked as a pair fought without devotion to a specific weapon. Maces, swords, arrows, and shields were thrown from the two attackers.

They dodged items as a never-ending sea of objects were projected into the crowd. One of the daggers sliced through the feather of a nearby being. The angel cried out and cradled his wing close to his chest. I had yet to feel pain and therefore believed the angel had not either, but angels could experience fear of being destroyed or damaged.

When my focus returned to the dwelling pair, I noticed the enemies became friends as their targets shifted from each other to those around them.

"Are you upset?" one of the new friends asked me. "You paired us to fight against one another, and we changed our task."

"It was changed for the better; therefore, I have no complaint. I applaud you taking the initiative and giving yourself authority." I stayed around the exterior of the room while the group practiced with each other. Adding them to the legion I had directed into Heaven the first day, I determined to strengthen my following.

I encouraged them to try new things and to be brave by saying, "Your unknown skills could become a great power, making you stronger and happier than ever before. You could experience satisfaction beyond measure. Branch out and use weapons other than what Elohim gave you."

"But, does not God know what is best?" asked the one with the staff.

"Possibly, but if you have never wielded a sword, how could He know if you would be better or worse?" I asked.

Many heads nodded. A look of wonder came into their eyes.

I continued, "Test and see for yourself what feels right."

With a shaking fist, he put down his staff and selected a bow. A flaming arrow hung from the string. He brought the cord to his cheek and aimed. The arrow shot instantly into the middle of a wooden shield, which burst into flames.

"Well done." I took a deep breath and blew out the fire. "It appears you have another option. Aren't you glad you tried an alternative?"

"Yes, I am," he admitted. "My name is Uriel."

"Good for you," I said. "I am Lucifer."

"I know," Uriel said.

I grinned knowing my name had spread beyond my followers.

Thousands of angels rushed to the armory, anxious to try weapons they had never considered using before. Leading them filled me with excitement. God had made a good selection when He chose me to create an army.

"Be merciful to each other as you try out new equipment," I instructed, feeling confident in my leadership. Elohim used Cassiel to help them learn from the weapon He selected and then Jehovah brought me in to help their skills grow.

Mixed throughout the duels, I saw Michael. His dark gray armor and wings made him harder to see, but the thick gold lining gave away his location. He wielded a sword like no other. Thirty pairs of duels circled him, and he battled one angel after another.

Many angels took notice of the fight. They clapped and chanted with excitement.

"Be easy on each other," I instructed. "I do not want to lose another today."

"You should have taken your own advice before destroying Cassiel," Michael said his voice deep with emotion. "My friend, what you did was disgusting." He continued to fight those around him. His movements slowed, and his breathing appeared labored.

"Mercy! Mercy! Mercy!" The crowd shouted, echoing Michael's sentiment.

No one said a word during my battle with Cassiel, but I felt their attention. Their mantra followed my command and filled me with a strange mixture of pride and jealousy. When I slayed their leader, I took his place.

What did they see in Michael? Could he supersede me as the greater warrior?

Following the advice of the crowd, when the angel could have stuck Michael down, he showed him leniency. I didn't want weak fighters. They needed to be brave and courageous.

Knowing he would not harm Michael made the once awe-inspiring duel less interesting.

The green fog of Dumah circled the feet of Michael's opponents.

"Let them be," I told him.

"Who are you?" Dumah asked.

"I am Lucifer."

"In whose authority do you command me?" Dumah's green mist drifted my direction.

"My own authority," I answered. I didn't want to appear frightened, but I also could not afford to be stupid and become a statue. I floated back from his fog.

His eyes narrowed on his already thin face, and his four wings carried him in a different direction. I hoped he retreated out of respect. I could have used Jehovah's name since I had His authority to create an army, but I wanted to know Dumah's reaction. Why would God create something with such a strange gift?

What became of the angel he'd turned into stone? I fluttered through the coliseum in search of the statue, but found no one.

Instinctually, I found myself floating toward the ground. Most of the action came from above, so I didn't understand my curiosity. I heard a strange sound. Two angels fought against one another, neither with weapons or armor. I didn't know why someone refused to use the available equipment.

The wings on the two angels' back were twice their height. Their plumage started thin, and as they drew closer to the ground, they widened to the size of my hand. One angel held the other to the ground. Neither wore shirts, and both had shaggy blond hair, reminding me of Phanuel. They could be confused for each other.

To the right of the pair stood the statue I had been searching for. The angel's muscles remained flexed with the war ax over his head. As I approached a fog lifted from the gray stone, I felt the presence of the Holy Spirit rather than confusion and knew it to be the source of the Fog.

Gray vapor swirled around the statue blurring the image. In the next breath, the statue vanished along with the Holy Spirit. Where did it go?

I looked to the wrestling angels, and it appeared they saw nothing unusual since their fight continued. The angel on bottom wrapped his legs around his opponent, flipping him to the side. A shout escaped his throat as they each tried to overtake the other. For a moment, I recognized Phanuel. He refused to use a weapon.

For someone as peaceful and calm as him, he also was stubborn. He needed further direction and leadership.

I would choose for him. Fluttering along the walls, I judged the many options. Phanuel's meekness made him seem unsuited for war. The shields varied in size and shape, all gold and encrusted with gems. They looked beautiful. The muscles Phanuel carried along his back and arms appeared sturdy and gave him the ability to master anything.

Thinking about his swift movements and agility, I felt confident he would not want something so bulky and cumbersome as a large shield. A spear or javelin had appeal. Not many of the warriors used that weapon. I looked them over. The silver-steel reflected off my light. Next to them stood golden arrows.

Would Phanuel be a coward to shoot from afar?

For some reason, I cared what others thought of him. As part of my army, I wanted him well trained. His ability would reflect on me as a leader. So, of course, his behavior mattered, and I wanted the best. I could see him as an expert archer, striking arrows through the tiniest of holes in his opponent's armor, the same as I had to Cassiel because I'd train him to do so.

In my mind, I saw the wounded angels tumbling into Zophos. It had been a strange area with dark smoke creating pillars and architecture resembling a dwelling place. In many ways, Zophos was the opposite of the glowing palace. The gloom made Zophos peaceful. However, the fire burning of Maalik's hair filled the air with a sulfurous odor.

I trembled thinking about the vision. Who were those who suffered? Was the hallucination an unavoidable prophecy? Or, was the vision a warning and something I could prevent from happening? The images needed to stop permanently so the dream could never be seen again.

With many mighty troops, I could do anything. My army would reign victoriously! But over what? Competing against God? Or worse, against each other, fighting to the end. What was this training for? The need for soldiers didn't make sense.

I selected a longbow made of acacia wood and a quiver of arrows. I felt confident Phanuel would like my choice and flew back at a rapid pace. My light reflected off the other pieces of armor like sparks as I shot back to the ground. The tiny lights drew the attention of others, and they lowered with me.

On the floor of the coliseum arms and legs moved rapidly and appeared similar to the point where I could not tell who they belonged to. The uncertainty made knowing when to feel celebratory difficult. A strong hand grabbed onto the throat of the other. The angel gasped for air. I had never thought of breathing as a necessity. What could be happening? I peered closer.

The difficulty in breathing wasn't due to strangulation but, the crushing air pipe, which would sever the head of the helpless angel. The dominate being's back and shoulders flexed as he continued to squeeze the existence out of his opponent.

I could not distinguish Phanuel from the other one. Was he dying or doing the killing? My instincts told me the gentle angel I'd seen multiple times would never physically take the life of another.

Without a moment to spare, I drew my sword and slashed the blade through the back of the attacking angel.

CHAPTER SEVEN

Through faith we understand that the worlds were framed by the word of God, so that things which are seen were not made of things which do appear.

- Hebrews 11: 3 (KJV)

At any other moment, stabbing an angel in the back would have been cowardly and unjust but, as the attacker disappeared, I looked into the grateful face of my friend.

Phanuel gasped frantically on the dark marble floor.

"Luc!" Michael's eyes narrowed, and his arms crossed over his armored chest. Disapproval radiated from him, though he said only my name.

"What?" I asked, sliding my sword into its sheath.

"Have you heard?" Michael asked.

Was I to be reprimanded again for destroying multiple angels?

"I did nothing wrong! Last time I was summoned to the Throne Room, I made a mistake. Not this time. Saving Phanuel's existence was the right thing to do, and I wouldn't hesitate to slay another again if necessary."

"Neither would I." Michael continued with urgency in his voice. "I was not speaking about that. More is happening on Earth."

"So?" I asked.

"You were there before. I thought you would want to see the changes."

"Thank you, Michael," I said, thinking of the splendor captured within space and feeling confident He could not create anything more amazing.

"Do you know what Jehovah is doing?" Phanuel asked. His voice sounded hoarse and weak.

I wanted to bring back the other angel so I could have the pleasure of eradicating the monster again for hurting Phanuel. Why did Elohim not give such a gentle creature a weapon or something with which to defend himself? Could He not see how much help my friend required? Maybe, I needed to show Him.

"I have heard rumors of other things with the ability to fly," Uriel answered. He had multiple robes over one arm and his staff in his other hand.

Belligerence rose within me causing my pulse to quicken. It was a new feeling and different, but pleasing. A righteous anger.

Phanuel sprung from the floor like the altercation with the other angel had never happened. A crinkle of his lower right wing was the only indication of the conflict. The flapping appendage glimmered from my glow, revealing a mist that strengthened the injury. Based on how quickly the wing repaired, in less than an hour, the evidence would dissolve away. The wing would return to its glittering splendor.

Was the Spirit causing Phanuel's body to renew? Could He mend the broken? Our God was a healer. Interesting.

Elohim's voice echoed from the halls of heaven. "It is good."

God had said the same at the creation of the stars, moon, and sun. Also, for the plants along the ground and the waters separated to construct land. Maybe, He said the same when He made me. I had not heard His words. I wished I had. Hearing the accolades would have pleased me, as well as the other angels.

"Come! Let's go see!" Phanuel's face glowed with excitement.

Michael glanced at the forgotten bow and quiver in my hand.

"Wait, Phanuel. I want you to begin using these." I handed him the weapons. "Keep them with you at all times."

He hesitated, the tip of his finger touching the acacia wood. "It's beautiful."

"I'll do my best to keep you safe, but I can't always protect you," I said.

"Your best is good enough for me." Phanuel returned the bow and quiver to their location.

I wanted him to reconsider, but also felt pleased by his faith in me.

"When I return, I will practice with the bow," said Phanuel. "I'll then consider whether to continue its usage."

"Fair enough," Michael declared.

"I agree," I said.

Phanuel grinned, an expression Michael and I returned. From day one, we traveled throughout Heaven together, learning our names and feasting in the banquet hall. Spending time with them had become a pleasure.

Looking around, I noticed several thousand angels surrounding me. Did they wait for me to decide on the new additions on Earth? If I decided to stay here, would they do the same?

I paused to consider my options. Being a positive example would bring more in my inner circle. Having a multitude would strengthen my army.

"Let's go," I declared.

God was building up to something on Earth, and I needed to know what. I shot through the golden gates directly to the blue and green planet. Two legions of angels followed me. Once we flew through the sphere's atmosphere, the gravitational pull brought us the rest of the way. With my wings outstretched, I glided through the air.

On my left and right, smaller creatures with vibrant feathers joined me. They resisted the pull toward land and remained in the sky. One, with white down, reminded me of the Spirit when He perched on Jehovah's shoulder.

I traveled the globe and found birds of every color. Some had the complete rainbow displayed along their body. Some of the birds were suited for cold temperatures, while others preferred warmer weather. They could travel to remain in their preferred climate.

"They are intelligent," Phanuel whispered.

"Their beauty is amazing," Michael said.

I shrugged. It bothered me that he had never complimented my appearance. Certainly, I was more attractive than some dull birds.

"Is this all He created?" I asked.

"I heard rumors of creatures under the waters," Uriel answered.

The flying animals were colorful and creative, but didn't impress me the way the stars had, or the way vegetation settled into place. Maybe if I had been able to watch these animals form, the creatures would seem more spectacular.

"Praise God!" Phanuel sang.

The birds chirped along with him. Somehow, they knew the same song. The unison perplexed me. Who taught the fowl the melody?

"Now, that is amazing." Michael waved to the birds, who fluttered as they sang.

"Perhaps to you." I shook my head. "To me, it seems redundant to have creatures with the ability to fly."

"What about the music?" Uriel asked.

"God taught the birds to praise him? If I did the same, would you consider the behavior to be extraordinary?" I asked.

Michael shook his head.

"I would," Phanuel said. His response didn't surprise me. I felt his devotion. His loyalty had grown significantly since saving him. Though his salvation had been dramatic, it had also been easy. I had no doubt I could bring others along as well. One follower would build on another, and soon a grand army would be formed.

A bird came close to me, tweeting the same song. The creature's talons grazed my shoulder, and I shooed it away.

I understood why Jehovah taught his creation songs of worship. I would have done it, too, but feared the scorn of my followers. Michael demonstrated he wouldn't understand. What about the others?

I had skills the Lord didn't. The capacity to err wasn't the best, but it counted for something. The ability was the start of more. There could be countless other skills that have not been explored. Soon, that would change.

"As much as you'd like to believe it, Luc, you are not God," Michael said

I glared at him. "Of course, I am not. Nor do I want to be. Why set my standards so low?" I asked.

"Low?" Uriel's brow furrowed. The feathers of his wings ruffled in unspoken protest.

"Yes." My answer stunned them into silence. They needed time to come to the same conclusion as I did.

Following the flying creatures, we watched them build homes from small twigs and needles from the pines. I understood their desire to live amongst the trees. The rich aroma filled the air, and we paused to enjoy the woodsy perfume.

"What is it you appreciate about God?" I asked.

I had Uriel's attention with my question but, he said nothing.

"God is good," offered Phanuel.

"We are all good," Michael said.

I nodded, pleased I wasn't the only one who thought so. I was marvelous and assumed the other angels were also.

A pause lingered between us until finally, Uriel added, "God is our Creator."

"That is true, but what if He creates something that shouldn't be?" I asked.

"Like what?" Phanuel asked

"Something not great," I answered.

They frowned.

"That seems unlikely," Phanuel said.

"We've been given these weapons, or at least most of us." I gestured to Phanuel. "Does it bother you that you weren't given anything?"

Phanuel thought for a long moment, and I wondered if he would answer. If he said no, there'd be proof he didn't like something God had done, or in this case didn't do.

"I think the weapons are beautiful, and some are creative with the lightning and fire coming from them. I get pleasure from looking at them. But, I do not believe they are for me," answered Phanuel.

"What about their purpose?" I asked. "Are we meant to fight each other? Is good destroying good the right thing? Shouldn't one side be the opposite?"

"I've been wondering the same thing," Michael said.

"I hope not," Phanuel said.

Michael and I nodded in agreement.

The sword and shield Michael carried matched his dark gray and gold outlined wings same as the armor along his chest and legs. The pieces paired perfectly like they had been created as a set. My friend's coordinating equipment gave me the impression they were made for battle.

I wondered if Jehovah or Elohim had given Michael the task of assembling an army. If not, I needed to add Their neglect to my list of mistakes God had made. Should I ask Michael and risk revealing the task Jehovah had given me? I let the question linger within me as we wandered through the air of Earth.

Suddenly, the clouds parted. Elohim's voice cried out from heaven, "Be fruitful, and multiply, and fill the waters in the seas, and let fowl fill the earth!"

He had given these creatures the ability to procreate! They have become their own Creators. Why would He do such a thing? The heat of resentment bubbled inside once again.

Michael's eyes narrowed, and his arms crossed over his chest with his mouth clamped tightly shut. It appeared I wasn't the only angel displeased with the new development.

Something leaped from the ocean. After the first, hundreds of silver scales jumped through the waves.

"Can we go with them?" Phanuel asked. "I want to see what's down there."

"I do not know," answered Michael.

"I've been in the ocean," I said.

"Really? That's great!" Phanuel didn't hesitate before diving through the water.

I felt the eyes of the legends who remained watching me. They had been mostly silent as we investigated the new flying creatures. I had forgotten about them. Many of their faces mirrored the same concern as Michael and myself. They looked to me for a solution which made me want to provide for them. I would not only be their leader but also minister to them.

"Elohim may have declared these creatures to be good, but I can see in your eyes you agree, it isn't. You are correct! God has made His first mistake today, and I predict it will not be His last."

"Luc," Michael whispered, shaking his head.

"No, listen to me. I am right about this. With each new day, He tries to do more and, as a result, He has become arrogant. What might He do next? The Trinity allowed us to be represented in the stars with the great warrior constellation. That was marvelous. But, today, we are mimicked throughout the air. We can go down in the sea and be distracted. We might forget the mockery taking place within the trees. I will not! I want you to remember with me! We—"

"Luc," Michael said again, rising between me and my listeners. "I think we should join Phanuel. He'll be waiting."

For the third time that day, anger boiled from within me. I didn't believe Michael cared about Phanuel. He only used him as an excuse to interrupt. Had we been alone, I would have scolded him but, for the sake of the crowd, I simply nodded.

"Of course. I would not want him getting lost out in the deep blue sea," I said, flying directly in front of the sun. My light cast down on everything. "Come, join me!"

I spiraled down an invisible staircase, plunging into the cold ocean. Small bubbles formed all around as thousands of angels followed me. My light provided the glow to see an assortment of fish, most of them the length of my arm, or shorter and full of colors. One had a royal blue body with fins which spread out into yellow, orange, and pinks.

"It's so smooth." Michael's fingers slid along the twisting body of a bright coral fish.

Hundreds of angels did the same, and I didn't like them acknowledging Michael's example. I was supposed to be their teacher.

A group of thin oval creatures were barely visible within the dark water. Drawing closer my light found their smooth sides flap like wings through the ocean. The pectoral fin slipped through my hand with ease until reaching its tail where a barb lifted from the ray's body.

"Proceed with caution," I said to my followers.

"It is because of your light we can see the danger."

I felt the gratitude and devotion of those around me strengthen.

"Stay with me, and I will protect you."

I swam further joined by my legions. My wings struggled to move me through the water, and my clothing dragged with weight. However, my arms and legs took over and guided me to the next astounding show deep within the ocean.

Massive groups of sparkling fish swam through beautiful reefs of purple, light blue, lime green, and orange. The reefs were a bizarre assortment of textures.

Guided by my light, thousands of angels stayed close as we explored the deep waters. The further we went, the larger the creatures became. Grandness was something I had grown accustomed too. I saw many massive things within the golden gates of heaven, but the sealife were bigger.

How did Jehovah continue to amaze me and the rest of the angels? My followers were all smiles, and I heard their murmurs of excitement in my mind. Despite Him being worthy of adoration, I didn't join in their praise to God.

While swimming with the fishes and two legions of angels, I felt perplexed by God. Why did He focus His energy on Earth? He had the great palace in the sky to keep us content and happy. The food provided a change and nice assortment of flavors. Many angels enjoyed removing the produce from the branches or vines and bringing them to the banquet hall. The vegetation brought new sweet smells and many vibrant colors but weren't better than the gems throughout the heavens.

God filled the waters and air, but there seemed to be a large space neglected. Land. Maybe the ground was for us to enjoy.

My head broke through the surface of the waters, surprised to find the sky to be filled with stars. Darkness covered most of the Earth, and I liked the gloom. The moon and I reflected light on those around us.

"I have yet to find Phanuel," Michael said.

"The ocean is large, but there are no dangers to him. I don't think he'll get lost," I said.

"I would very much like to return to heaven. If he has gone there, I will send word," offered Barachiel. I hadn't noticed him within my followers. There were too many to see them all which pleased me. Barachiel's long layers of colorful robes didn't handle water well, which made his desire to leave understandable.

"You may go," Michael directed.

I narrowed my eyes at him for commanding someone under my leadership. He will not take them from me!

Barachiel and a thousand others returned to heaven. Though they flew further away, our connection remained. I grew proud of the army assembled around me. Seeing them practice in the coliseum, I knew they were skilled with their weapons. Some had selected multiple tools and used them as well. I wished there was a way to get Cassiel back. It troubled me that I had defeated someone so powerful, but being triumphant felt wonderful. I enjoyed being victorious and wanted to continue.

I rose from the water along with my followers. Moisture dripped from our clothing, drying from the wind. Though I felt the cold, the temperature didn't bother me. I flew through the open air, deep in thought.

Initially, Phanuel being on my side appeared to be a weakness, but my compassion toward him allowed others to respect and follow me. His fragility made him an asset rather than a hindrance. I didn't know where he had gone, but I was confident if something happened to him, I'd sense the loss.

Dumah's green fog drifted over the ocean. He struggled with his two set of wings while within the water, and now droplets sprayed about as he tried to free the moisture from his wings. Part of me feared him, the same way I had Maalik and his sulfur builders. At the same time, I wanted them on my side.

Why did I feel the need to have sides? Some type of battle seemed like such an obvious reality. Michael mentioned he thought the same. I took that as confirmation I remained on the right path. The golden angel was strong and intelligent. I felt honored to call Michael my friend and ally.

"What makes you certain Phanuel is well?" Michael asked.

I paused for a moment, unsure of expressing my theory of loyalty. However, another experience would lead to confirmation and that had strong appeal.

"I can feel that he's fine," I answered.

"As can I."

Did that mean Phanuel was loyal to Michael, also? I needed to keep a close eye on my warrior friend. Maybe he received a different message than me. It could be voiced by God rather than by Phanuel. I wanted to know more.

"If you can feel him, then why question his safety? Do you think something's wrong?" I asked.

"The feeling I have is faint. I know he exists, but whether he is well or not I am not certain," Michael said.

"I'm sure he appreciates your concern. Your interest would mean a great deal to him, as it does to me." I assumed other angels felt the faith of their comrade and not only Michael and myself.

Having confirmation regarding the connection with the other angels filled me with courage. In contrast, I wondered why I found following Jehovah so difficult. Rather than awe-inspiring, God had become a rival. His success and praise brought resentment.

I remembered the hesitation from those with me when we learned this new stage of creation could procreate. The time had come to gather my resources, and see what we could do together. I needed to discover my abilities and show these new skills to my followers. They would see I was the most powerful.

CHAPTER EIGHT

"...Be fruitful and multiply."
- Genesis 1:22, 1:28, 8:17, 9:1 and 9:7

In the distance, the waves of the ocean crept up the shoreline only to recede into the depths. The salty air filled my chest, and the rhythmic movement sounded peaceful. As the sun peeked from the East, brilliant oranges and pinks reflected off the clouds.

The host of Heaven around me remained silent as God painted the morning sky. I had never seen anything like it.

"It's truly awe-inspiring," mumbled Michael, but I clung onto my frustrations. The painting in the sky wouldn't make me forget the mockery flying through the trees.

Michael and another angel sang.

"I will exalt you, my God, and bless your name forever and ever.
Great is the Lord, and greatly to be praised.
His greatness is unsearchable.
On the glorious splendor of your majesty and on your wondrous works, I will contemplate."

The songs had become elaborate with the passing of each new day.

As I listened, my displeasure grew. I didn't like what they were saying. Yes, God did amazing things, but their devotion seemed extreme.

The song continued.

"Our Lord is gracious and merciful, slow to hostility and abounding in steadfast love.
The Lord is good to all, and his mercy is over all He has made."

Those lyrics gave me pause. God showed compassion on me and great kindness when I was reprimanded in the Throne Room. Why did I not feel the same gratitude as the other angels?

As they sang, God filled the sky with colors. The beautiful picture encouraged the host, and the birds joined in song.

"All Your works shall give thanks to You, O Lord, and all Your creation shall bless you!
They speak of Your glory and tell of Your power, to make known Your mighty deeds, and the glorious splendor of Your domain.
You open your hand and satisfy the desire of every living thing."

My desires had not been satisfied. Maybe theirs had been but, rather than feeling content, I wanted them to aspire for more. I could become their champion and make them better in the process.

I had finally heard enough! In some ways, they were right, and He deserved their praise at this moment but wasn't always appropriate.

"What if Jehovah did something we didn't like?" I didn't mean to say the words out loud. They were floating inside my mind, and that was where I intended them to stay, but instead, they leaped out.

"That is not possible," Michael said.

"Yes, it is," came the deep voice of Abaddon.

I had not seen him since exploring the darkness of Earth's shadow and didn't realize he had been included in the legion following me through the sea. He might have joined us as we floated above the ocean, letting the water drip from our clothing and wings. He could have been enjoying the gloom when God interrupted his pleasure to give us a painting in the sky.

"Why question His provision?" Michael asked.

"I am not the only one who has done so." Abaddon gestured to those around us, his other hand remaining outstretched toward me.

Feeling unease being near Abaddon, the frightened legion retreated from his attention.

My eyes narrowed, and I wondered how he would have such knowledge. "Do we have to follow Him if we disagree with His decisions?" I asked.

"I am my own being," Abaddon answered.

"I belong to Elohim," Michael said.

I nodded, but my options perplexed me. Was our response praise if there wasn't something opposite to compare the greatness to? Did I want to belong to Elohim? Being my own, like Abaddon mentioned, had merit.

Watching the sun's glow lift the darkness, the light revealed the world's beauty. In the distance Jehovah walked across the waves. The ocean splashed against his white robes. A murmur of excitement rumbled through my followers.

They remembered the great wonders I described as the Creator divided the seas from the land and made vegetation grow. My curiosity matched theirs, wondering what God would do next.

Once standing on dry land, the Lord scooped soil into his hand. He said, "Let the earth bring forth the living creatures after his kind, cattle, and creeping things, and beast of the earth."

Jehovah took a deep breath and blew into the dust. The dirt swirled around him like a brown funnel. Bouncing from the soil came small animals with long, floppy ears and short cotton tails. A large beast with thick black fur stood on its back legs and roared. Another with smooth hair and horns charged into existence.

The angels gasped, and I joined them as hairless, scaly animals crawled from the dust. Some of them were tiny and others as large as trees, shaking the earth with each heavy step. More things than I could imagine galloped, waddled, and prowled from the dusty funnel.

"What are you?" Abaddon asked small creatures scampering about and squeaking to one another.

Their tiny bodies trembled and their voices were so high I almost could not hear them. "I do not know," they answered together.

"I'll find out," I said.

"How?" Michael asked.

"You'll see." I refused to show them my nervousness as I approached the swirling cloud of dirt.

What if as I entered as a vicious creature leaped out on me? Could I be injured by their sharp teeth and claws? I pushed aside my concerns and stepped into the funnel, feeling the apprehension of my followers as I disappeared.

Inside, I found Jehovah with beasts around him. One had four furry legs and a lengthy tail with long light brown mane around its face. The animal laid in His lap. Rubbing against the animal's fur was a creature with a puffy white coat, skinny legs, and hoofed feet.

Jehovah whispered to them, smiling and touching His creation gently.

Why does He not gaze on me with the same compassion? Certainly, I'm better than meek animals.

Then the creatures whispered praise to their Creator. Maybe that was why Jehovah prefers them over me. How much apparent pride could one Being have? Why have so many avenues led to the same results? All screamed out their praise or declared how awesome He was.

Enough is enough!

Jehovah looked at me the same way He did the animals, though he heard my thoughts. Now, He gave me attention. It was too late! I didn't care if He knew I didn't like Him. Plenty of others told Him how amazing He was; I didn't need to be included.

"Lucifer," Jehovah said. I made eye contact with Him but didn't speak. "Is there something you came here to ask?"

"I thought you knew all things."

"I do."

He continued making new animals from the dirt swirling around us, like my presence changed nothing.

One of the beasts caused the funnel to expand as it filled the space with its long trunk and big flapping ears. I ducked as the animal bellowed like a trumpet and stomped out to join the other creatures.

"Answer my question without me asking," I shouted over the ruckus.

"You shouldn't test the Lord your God," He said.

"Yes I should! You need to get used to me asking because there will be more testing. Quit stalling and answer my question!"

Jehovah's eyes narrowed.

I had angered Him, and I felt pleased.

"You want to know the names of these creatures and the ones who came before them," Jehovah said.

"Yes."

"Their names are not for me to give," Jehovah answered.

"I don't understand." I spat out the words and glared. Why did God perplexed me so much. It must bring Him joy to fester with my emotions. It was the only explanation for His constant annoyance. "It doesn't matter. I don't care. Enjoy your Earth and the ridiculous things you've added to it."

"The desire for knowledge is strong for you, Lucifer. You are intelligent, crafty and swift." Jehovah stood, walking closer to me. A long reptile slithered down His arm and onto my shoulder. I grimaced as its tongue darted from between sharp fangs and threw the thing out of the swirling funnel.

Jehovah continued, "Be careful you do not rely too heavily on what you do not know. It can be dangerous to storm forward to things that come to you easily."

"I'm not lazy!" I countered.

"I know."

"Do you really? Because these critters seem too problematic for you to manage on your own. And I'm more complicated than them."

"Be patient. More is yet to come."

The swirling brown cloud lifted, leaving pairs of animals in every size, shape, and color imaginable. Jehovah spoke out, encouraging them to be fruitful and multiply, the same He had said to the birds of the air and the creatures within the sea.

I felt questions forming in the mind of my legion. They wanted to know what Jehovah had told me about His creation. I didn't have an answer unless I named them myself. I could not return without knowing the truth.

What was truth? I wondered if Jehovah had given me an answer, would that automatically make it true? He seemed hesitant to answer like He didn't know.

I had stumbled across something God didn't know. He wasn't all-knowing! That was even better to share than the names of insignificant animals.

Jehovah closed His eyes, and His lips moved but, I heard nothing as the swirling cloud carried us. Through the dirt funnel, I saw us land in a desert with little growth and no water in sight. In every direction, the horizon displayed layers of earth stacked high to form brown mountains. Jehovah stepped from the brown cloud. Not wanting to be left behind, I exited with Him.

The churning soil came together to form a white dove, which approached Jehovah to sit on His shoulder. I had been standing in the presence of the Holy Spirit. How did I not know that?

I assumed the twirling funnel to be Jehovah performing miracles and being the amazing Creator he was, instead the channel was the Fog and Jehovah working together. I wondered what would happen if Elohim became involved.

Jehovah smiled at me and looked like He wanted to say something, but he waited. It was the same thing he told me to do; to have patience. Then His gaze lifted to the sky.

Suddenly, a trumpet blasted. The sound drew my attention along with the rest of the heavenly hosts'. Gabriel dressed in layers of white had his sword remained sheathed at his side, and his straight blond hair fluttered in gusts from the wings of the other angels. He played the same melody of the birds. A chorus of voices sang, and a full brass band came together in the sky.

I didn't have to see the cloud coming out of Heaven to know Elohim had left the Throne Room to enter Earth's atmosphere. A thick vapor floated through the rows within the mountain.

The dove remained on the shoulder of Jehovah as Elohim came closer. Thunder echoed from every corner of Earth, and lightning danced in all direction.

I clenched my hands into fists to keep my fingers from quivering. My wings kept me afloat inches above the ground. Determination kept me from fleeing in terror. If anyone asked if I were scared, I would have said no. That response would have been the first of many lies.

The mountains filled with smoke, billowing in the wind. The Earth trembled, and the rocks cried out in praise. Unable to help myself, I bowed. My Creator had come.

God said, "Let Us make man in our image, after our likeness: and let them have dominion over the fish of the sea, the fowl of the air, the cattle, and over the Earth."

His words sounded as if He had spoken a language I didn't understand. That wasn't possible, since I could read and knew every dialect. For some absurd reason, God wanted to make something in Their likeness.

No! That could not happen.

There was no reason to put rulers on Earth when there was *us*. We could do whatever He wanted. I had gathered two legions of warriors and had taught them their weapons. All we needed was an assignment, and we'd be ready!

Jehovah lifted the soil into his hands. His head bowed as if blessing the ground. The Dove joined with the Cloud and wrapped around Jehovah's hands, lifting the dirt. From the dust, God formed two legs, a torso, two arms and a head. The face appeared beautiful and peaceful with his eyes and mouth closed.

I had to stop this creation from happening, but I didn't know how. My brilliant mind felt sluggish and impaired. In complete horror, I watched.

All together, God took a deep breath and exhaled into the nostrils of man. His creation breathed and became a living being. I wanted to hate him, but he was too perfect. His muscled arms and chest reminded me of Phanuel. Only the man didn't have wings.

I felt my angels' amazement at the splendor of God's creation. Could they not see how devastating this was? We were being replaced and the idiots didn't understand!

I will fly into the heavens and help them to see. Their eyes will be opened, and I will be their rescuer!

Fire raging within me; I shot back to the gates of heaven. The beauty of the golden streets and glittering gems meant nothing.

"Phanuel!" I shouted.

My voice echoed throughout the quiet halls. Most of the angels watched God make a fool of Themselves. I charged to the dark marbled room full of armor. Whoever remained to practice their skills was someone I wanted on my team.

Half a million of pairs sparred with one another. Precious metal tinged together, creating another song. Others aimed longbows at targets far in the distance. I heard the sound before seeing the electricity. Lightning danced as the fiery whip of Sammael attacked his opponent.

The traitor had gone to the Throne Room to inform Elohim of my mistake. Sammael's wings arched around his body, protecting him as the worthless straps he called clothing tangled around his midsection.

I began to approach when Phanuel stopped me.

"Lucifer, sir, you called?"

"Thank you for coming." I took a deep breath to stifle my anger. "Do you know what has happened on Earth?"

"Yes, God has created man!" His face appeared radiant from my light but also had a glow that was his own. His purity and innocence made him special. He clapped his hands and continued to praise God.

"Be quiet!" I demanded. "It's not good."

"That can not be." Phanuel's face fell like countering me hurt him.

"It's difficult to explain, but I need you to trust me. I want you to remain on Earth. Open yourself fully to me and be my witness. Through your devotion, I'll see and know everything you experience."

Phanuel nodded and stood straighter, exhibiting the pride he felt at being given such an extraordinary task. "I will tell you everything. After man's creation, the Lord God took him to a great garden to take care of everything. The nursery has four streams winding through the land and trees of every kind like you described."

I remembered the garden from the third day. One tree seemed defective, for the leaves withered quickly, with the foliage turning from green to red and yellow and then leaving the tree once brown and dead. Then new growth returned shortly for the cycle of life to go on.

Phanuel continued, "Then God commanded the man, saying, 'Of every tree of the garden you may freely eat, but of the Tree of the Knowledge of Good and Evil, thou shalt not eat of it; for in the day that you eat thou shalt surely die.'"

"It's getting worse!" I declared. "Now, God has put conditions on His creation."

The young angel's head shook. He needed time to see what I already did. The Trinity made an obvious mistake.

"Go, and keep me posted," I instructed.

"Yes, sir!" Phanuel bowed for a moment and then bolted from sight. I felt his mind as he settled back on Earth.

My focus returned to Sammael and his duel. The electric whip he willed reached out to someone, barely missing their long, bronze wings. Sammael's flapping appendages wrapped around his shoulders like arms and the six-foot length feathers came down to his feet.

The full brass wings of his opponent appeared familiar, but I didn't recognize the weapon. The tool appeared heavy like a two-handed sword, but the tip wedged out like an ax. As I approached, the weapon glowed light blue. When Sammael's whip connected with the special sword, purple sparks jumped from the contact.

My light reflected off the angel's bronze wings and short copper hair. I wanted him to win and take out my former accuser. Sammael could get what he deserved. I didn't know what became of the destroyed angels, but that didn't matter.

The two angels danced as their weapons struck against each other. Neither had shields. If mine could be used to help defeat Sammael, then I'd gladly offer it.

"Friend!" I called out.

Sammael's white hair shimmered from my light as he faced me. He smiled. I guessed he thought I had yelled at him. What a fool.

The other angel turned and I recognized Cassiel. How did he return? Where had he disappeared to?

CHAPTER NINE

And God saw everything that he had made, and behold, it was very good. And the evening and the morning were the sixth day."
- Genesis 1:31

"Lucifer!" Phanuel called. "You will not believe what has happened!" He paused breathlessly like he had flown as fast as he could to return with an urgent message.

All the duels came to a halt. The angels gathered close to hear what he had to say. The situation reminded me of when I had shared my experience with those in the banquet hall. My words were consumed faster than the delicious fruits spread across the wide acacia table.

"What is it?" I asked. I stood closer to him to make it apparent Phanuel had come specifically to me. I would not allow him to steal the other angels' attention.

The young angel took a breath, his excitement making him more charming. "The man, the one God formed from the dust."

"I could have guessed, since there is only one man."

"Right." Phanuel averted his eyes for a moment. "Well, uh, he named the animals."

"Why?" Cassiel asked.

"I do not know. The Lord God brought them to Adam and as they crossed his path, the man named them," Phanuel answered.

"Elohim gave us our names and Jehovah gave names to the stars in space." My voice echoed off the dark marble pillars. "Why? Why did They give such responsibility and dominion to a helpless creature?"

I felt a righteous indignation well up inside and erupt in the form of a battle cry.

Phanuel crouched back from my rage.

His voice came in the form of a whisper. "I believe the man was looking for a helpmate."

I sneered, glaring at no one in particular. "What an idiot! Why look for a companion amongst animals who already had theirs."

Laughter bubbled inside of me from the same source as the anger. This time, I wasn't alone. Thousands of angels joined me in mockery of the one too ignorant to know any better.

Phanuel turned away, his body bristling from our snickering.

"Thank you for this report," I said. "Go, and return when there is another enlightening development."

"I will, sir." Phanuel's eyes didn't reach mine as he flew from the room.

If I had embarrassed him, that wasn't my intention. I had almost told him so, but his retreat had been too fast. Instead, the blue glow from Cassiel's weapon caught my attention.

"What is this?" I asked.

"Elohim gave it to me. The weapon is to help me to know good," Cassiel answered.

Sammael joined another duel, leaving myself and Cassiel to our conversation. Maybe they had already discussed the events that brought my warrior friend back, which was why the accuser didn't stay for additional details. Or maybe, Sammael didn't care, but I did and wanted further understanding.

"Good from evil?" I asked. "Like the tree planted in the garden."

"Yes," Cassiel said.

"According to Phanuel, the man will die if he eats from that tree. Is that what happened to you?" For a moment I thought of apologizing for destroying him, but he was fine. I did no real harm to him.

"For the man, it is separation from God. When you ravished me, it was similar in that we were no longer together, but I arrived at the feet of Elohim. There, I was given insight like my eyes had been fully opened."

"Use your weapon! Do this to me," I commanded, lifting his glowing blade to my throat.

Cassiel moved the sharp edge away from me. "There is no need. You have discovered the same knowledge on your own."

My theories about God's abilities, or lack of, were now confirmed. Most would have sought revenge on me. Instead, Cassiel seemed pleased by his newly acquired awareness.

"Thank you," I said.

Suddenly, Phanuel returned, but not in physical form. His mind opened fully to me, and I could see and hear everything he thought as if I were a witness.

From above my head, a vision of beautiful flowers bloomed within the garden. They weaved together to create a collection of colors and shapes to form a masterpiece mirroring the jewels across heaven. Through Phanuel, I smelled their sweet nectar. The four streams rushed over gems glittering in the sunlight.

The voice of the Lord God echoed through the trees saying, "It is not good that the man should be alone—"

I knew it! Before everyone the Trinity admitted their mistake. He made my task easy by demonstrating to everyone the absurdity of everything He had done.

"God should have lied to hide his fault," I mumbled.

"But that is something else the Lord can not do," countered Sammael. His duel, as well as the others, ceased.

"How pathetic." I laughed but didn't smile.

My angry eyes matched Cassiel's. We were alike in many ways, and I wondered if he saw the similarities.

"His truthfulness works against Him," I said.

"What do you suggest?" Cassiel asked.

"For God to make another as he did with the animals," I answered. "Is that not obvious?"

"It is," Sammael replied.

The vision continued. From above Adam laid on the soft grass. Cassiel and Sammael stared into space like I did, and I wondered if they saw the same images. I didn't believe Phanuel was as connected to them as he was to me. Where did their vision come from?

Maybe what I saw had nothing to do with my servant Phanuel and instead was a gift from the Holy Ones. They allowed us to see the activity on Earth. My preference was to believe everything I saw to have been something only for me. I didn't want God taking credit for *my* abilities.

Regardless of how the vision arrived, I watched.

Adam looked at peace, with his eyes and mouth closed and his muscled chest rising and falling with each breath. The Holy Spirit hovered over the body; His transparent form kept the man at rest.

Jehovah reached his hand to touch Adam's side. The tip of His finger sliced through the man's flesh.

A gasp ricocheted through heaven.

What is He doing?

He's hurting him!

Why?

I heard their questions and wondered the same.

"What other horrors must He be capable of?" I whispered.

"I do not know," mumbled Sammael.

I felt the bodies of my followers as they huddled closer to me. I'd protect them from God if the time came.

Not a drop of blood escaped from the man as God reached inside the body. Jehovah broke a bone from the man.

Again, Heaven gasped, and their confusion grew. For the first time doubts about God's character surfaced.

I felt the anxiety of those around me watching God damage His creation.

Would we be next?

Elohim closed Adam's wound.

The same glimmer of healing from the Holy Spirit on the man's body that had been on Phanuel's wing when it had been damaged. Fixing the injury didn't counter the fact God had unnecessarily harmed something He had made.

From the rib, God formed another human. The tan skin matched Adam's and had the same body structure except her arms and legs were elegantly crafted and less muscular. Also, the hips were wider, and her chest developed full breasts. Long black hair trailed down her smooth back. She was more beautiful than any other created thing.

My breath quickened followed by many feelings I had never experienced before and didn't understand. I had felt jealous of Michael's matching armor and irritation at Jehovah and anger. But suddenly, I wanted this creation with more passion and fervor than ever before.

"Mine..." I heard the echo before realizing the voice came from me.

"It is exquisite," Cassiel said.

The vision continued as Jehovah turned His masterpiece toward me. I felt drawn to every curve of the body standing before me. Then God became the ultimate betrayer as He brought His radiant creation to the man.

A low growl vibrated through the back of my throat. The same came from my followers.

Adam touched his side. He didn't appear to be in pain, but a thick scar raised above the surface of his skin. "This is now bone of my bones and flesh of my flesh," Adam said. "She shall be called 'woman,' for she was taken out of man."

"Well, isn't he creative," I mocked. It didn't take brilliance to come up with that name for her and put into question the intelligence of God's latest creation.

The lightning of Elohim rumbled within the garden. From the cloud, Father God placed smoky hands on the heads of the two humans blessing them.

"Be fruitful, and multiply. Replenish the earth, and subdue it. Have dominion over the fish of the sea, the fowl of the air, and over every living thing that moves upon the earth."

And just like that, the Lord gave *my* Earth to meaningless humans! Even the weakest of angels had cloth to cover their nakedness. But to the man and woman, God provided them nothing! But, at the same time, gave them everything.

We were supposed to enjoy the produce from the ground. We were supposed to take care of the animals. I was supposed to multiply my army and with it subdue the Earth!

As a unit, the Trinity lifted Themselves from the planet and reflected on their creation.

"It is very good," They declared.

"No, it *is* not!"

CHAPTER TEN

The pillars of Heaven tremble and are astonished at his reproof.
- Job 26: 11 (KJV)

The heavens became a buzz of activity as everyone had been given the same vision as myself. We watched together as I confirmed that God had made the worst decision of His existence.

"Lucifer, Lucifer!" Phanuel shouted, flying to my side, unaware I had been given sight to Earth.

"I already know." My anger bubbled, filling me with heat.

Phanuel paused to judge my reaction.

Crossing my arms over my chest, I waited for him to speak.

"God didn't make a mistake in the creation of one man, but rather wanted Adam to see for himself he needed a partner," Phanuel said. "The Trinity had already created male and female within the animal kingdom. It would make sense for Him to do the same for humans."

"You are missing the point. They shouldn't have created man at all. The Earth should have been for us."

"Maybe, you're right," said Cassiel.

"I'm sorry you feel that way." Phanuel's shoulders slumped in my direction. His face looked at me with urgency. He wanted a way to make me and God happy.

That was no longer possible.

"Phanuel, gather the legion who I led through Heaven on our first day. Cassiel, do the same for those who were here in the armory when you were defeated. It's time for my army to take back what is rightfully ours!"

The two angels bowed their heads and then left as fast as lightning. Those who saw the vision with me stayed close. I felt their anxiety and their wings trembled.

"Friends," I said. "I have something better in mind. God is holding you *all* back, and I have the ability to set you free. There will be no limit to your greatness. *We* are capable of amazing things, and those skills should no longer be hidden under Their shadow. Don't you think we deserve praise as well?" I thought of my legion and wanted what was best for them.

I smiled at Phanuel and Cassiel's quick return. It confirmed my follower's loyalty and made me stronger. I hoped my confidence made them tenacious as well.

I continued. "Together, we can do anything! You can develop your own powers. Find out what true holiness is about. Think of the possibilities. You praise God imagining Him being worthy of worship, but with your new abilities, you can make *Yourself* worthy and become greater."

Gabriel used his wings to lift himself over the massive crowd, his sword drawn. "Even at our best we can not be more supreme than God," Gabriel said, the typically peaceful angel squared his shoulders and rested his hand on the hilt of his weapon.

Cassiel nodded to Gabriel in agreement. "The Lord has done amazing things. We saw him form the planets and create space. On Earth, it is beautiful. If He has commandments for us to follow, we should obey. But, above all, we must respect the Lord our God."

"Imagine the possibilities." Phanuel's face glowed with wonder and awe. "If we carefully follow His commands, exactly as the Lord our God told us, then one day He will say we have done a great thing. That day will be amazing!"

I flew to the young angel's side. I wasn't offended by their loyalty to the Trinity. Phanuel wanted everything to be well and good. I could help him to see and know my ways were better.

From one side of the grand coliseum to the other, all filled with my followers. Their hands clenched around their weaponry and determination shot from their eyes. I could feel their need for retribution against God's latest creation, and I intended on giving it to them.

Gabriel shook his head. "Remember the Lord is holy and good. We can trust Him! He will keep His word and has shown

His love and kindness to all who love Him. We should not look at His punishment as being unfair. For He punishes those who hate Him!" Gabriel lifted his sword to me. "God will destroy Lucifer, and He will not be slow to punish those who follow him."

"Does that sound loving to you? Is that what a noble God should do?" I asked. "Why worship an all-or-nothing God when I can promise you better? We will be limitless."

"But, we also need to be good," countered Cassiel.

I felt the force of those following me, rock back and forth like the waves of the ocean. At Cassiel's words, I felt weak. I had not realized how much of my strength relied on my legion's support. I wanted them but now became aware I needed them.

"Was it good for God to slice open the side of man?" I asked.

"Yes, because then He created woman," smirked Sammael.

"God could have used the same dirt He made man from," I said. "There was no reason to harm His creation. God is cruel and dangerous. Friends, do not be deceived. If you want to remain good, then be good, but do so on your own terms. Do it because it makes *you* happy and not to bring someone else glory. Once you see your full potential, share this good news with everyone."

Phanuel's eyes lifted toward the Throne Room. I felt his questions. Why did They allow me to continue? It had been well-established God knew everyone's thoughts. I needed to answer my servant and many others who wondered the same thing.

I placed my hand on Phanuel. "This peaceful angel wants to know why They have given me the opportunity to share my message with others."

The crowd grew. Their eyes widen as it appeared I had the same abilities as God.

"Yes, friends. I know his thoughts." I smiled at Phanuel, who nodded in confirmation.

"Know this followers. As before, when I was summoned to the Throne Room, God will gather us together to make me a demonstration of what happened to those who defy Them. But, what if my words right now aren't any different than what They already believe. I am allowed to speak because They know I am right!"

A collective gasp echoed throughout the dark coliseum. Their voices mingled together whispering their agreement to each other.

"I am listening," Cassiel said.

"Thank you, my friend." I smiled at him and hoped he felt my appreciation the same way I could feel his. "Let us consider the creation of man. Do you realize your replacements will multiply on Earth? Once humans populate the land, then God will not have any purpose for you."

"It's not like we do anything," mumbled Sammael.

I circled him. He was my least favorite angel, but I offered my freedom to him as well as the rest of heaven.

"Sammael has an excellent point. I offer *you* a purpose. Something to do. I am completely impartial to who joins me."

"What do you want from us?" Phanuel stood taller, his gaze meeting mine.

Pride welled up inside of me as the dark grey armory brightened from my glory. The Holy Spirit floated through my audience and gathered its fog to be directly in front of me. I felt Elohim's anger as the pillars trembled and His thunder rumbled throughout heaven.

"Lucifer, come forth!" God said.

"It looks like I have somewhere to be. Come with me and you'll find freedom. Do not be afraid to be with me. Fear the Lord. He is great and powerful, but He doesn't really listen to you. I will listen. He's the stubborn one. I am a being of peace. Elohim is quick to anger. I am not. Let us go and make something for ourselves that will be stronger and greater than all. Greater!"

I felt powerful and strengthened as thousands of followers aligned themselves with me. Now was the moment to take my words and put them into action.

"Greater!" I heard echo throughout the heavenly realm. The sound was no longer my voice but of several millions chanting together. "Greater… Greater…"

"I'll come with you." Phanuel's head bowed in submission.

"I doubt you'll be the only one," I smirked. "We *are* greater! Let's go!" I unsheathed my sword and raised it over my head. "To the Throne Room! Either God goes, or we do!"

The last time I ascended the crystal staircase I knew I had done something wrong. The error was minor and a mistake I didn't mean to make. This time, I wasn't the one who had gone astray. I confidently placed one foot in front of the other, gaining courage with each step.

The stampede of my army followed my every move. Inside the Throne Room, Elohim and Jehovah sat in their usual place with the Holy Spirit hovering between them. The brightness and jeweled beauty of the surroundings didn't awe me in the same way the room had when I first arrived.

Before the Trinity laid a scroll, the ends glowed, giving the papyrus the ability to continue forever. Something being added to the room was different, but not overly surprising.

"What is that?" I asked.

"The Book of Life," answered Jehovah.

I would have asked what that meant, but I didn't care. What caught my attention was that we weren't alone.

It was like the walls of the Holy of Holies disappeared and all of the Heaven bore witness to our meeting.

"I told you," I whispered to Cassiel. "They want everyone to hear my message."

Cassiel nodded.

Previously, I found the audience humiliating, but not so this time. I had nothing to be ashamed of. I would hold the Trinity accountable for Their blunder.

"You called?" I smirked at Them.

I felt the respect from Cassiel and the curiosity of my legions. From day one, thousands had been under my care, and now I'd be their *savior*.

Hearing my thoughts, Jehovah turned his head to me.

I struck a nerve with that thought. I knew the many words inscribed upon the golden gate were the names of God. One of them was "Savior," but the description was inaccurate. God wasn't saving creation; he destroyed it all with man. They needed me. I would restore the proper order to the universe.

"Remove your weapons," Elohim commanded me.

I looked at the crystal sea. Last time, my shield had safely carried my sword, and I had no doubt that would be true again. But, I had no desire to follow God's will no matter how minor.

"I will not yield them," I replied.

There was a low rumble throughout the heavenly realm as I verbally and physically defied God. Whether the others were impressed or concerned, I could not tell. I hoped my behavior proved to my followers I'd be a better leader.

Suddenly, the floor of Heaven shook. My wings lifted me further from the ground and angels huddled together. The Crystal Sea, which surrounded the thrones, melted away. Bubbles formed and then turned to red lava. The hot molten flowed deeper, carving out the edges of the cavern. The intense heat caused my forehead to ache.

Zophos could now be seen from inside heaven.

I felt abandoned as the angels floated back from the dangerous precipice. I pitied them. My legions needed to know the hole was safe, and I'd never let harm come to them. The glow of the flowing fire revealed the smoky pillars which Maalik and his group had constructed.

The sulfur burned my nose. I brought one wing over my face for protection. Several did the same, but most used both of their wings leaving them vulnerable and weak.

"Lucifer, be gone!" Elohim said, and Jehovah pointed to the lava.

I joined the heavenly host in a collective gasp. The finality of God's judgment took me by surprise. The last time I had been here I had been shown mercy. Now, They were harsh and cruel.

"Pardon me, Holy One," Michael said. "Is it not proper to allow Lucifer to explain himself?"

"No!" Elohim thundered.

"Lucifer must go down into Zophos." Jehovah stood from his throne and pointed directly at me. "You have committed a terrible sin and have turned away from what I have commanded you to do."

"I have not! For how can I obey what I have not been taught?" I asked. "You never gave any commandments or told us how to worship. I don't know what sin is!"

"Maybe He didn't want to give you the idea," Gabriel said. "The Lord God is wise and gives us instruction for our protection."

"Shut your mouth!" I hissed at him. "Are you suggesting I am too weak to be told good from evil, and can not be trusted to choose good? Right now, as we speak, I am choosing what is right!" My voice echoed throughout Heaven as anger boiled through my body. I felt its heat warming me, which brought me comfort.

Good needed evil to be right. I provided that goodness. The heavenly host believed God to be great, all the time, but they were wrong. I needed to help them to see the error of their ways. They could come to me, and I'd open their eyes. I'd take them the way they were and lead them on a better path. One where they could create their own destiny and no longer be slaves to the will of the Trinity.

Jehovah clenched his fists as he spoke, "I have seen inside the heart of Lucifer. He is corrupt. He will continue to defy us and must be banished." His voice rumbled loudly.

I wasn't the only one angry. His emotion made Him insecure and out of control. I had hit another nerve. My confidence soared.

Michael bowed his head and stepped in front of the Trinity, kneeling before them. His sword and shield laid by his side and his face turned downward.

"I beg you, Lord my God, do not let your anger destroy what you have created," Michael said. "Do not allow us to look upon You and say, 'God did horrible things to His creation. That you planned Lucifer's destruction from the beginning.' Change your mind, and give him the chance to speak for himself. I have been by Lucifer's side as he sung praises to you. Would it not be better to redeem than to punish him? I, your servant Michael, beg for mercy, dear Lord."

A silent pause fell upon us as the Trinity considered Their options. The thunder and lightning under Elohim's throne softened as his anger subsided. "Lucifer, you may speak."

"I don't need mercy, for I have done nothing wrong." I floated high, looking down on the heavenly realm. "Today, a mere angel was able to change the mind of God. Is that who you want to serve? I think not. Friends, God opened the walls of the Throne Room so all may enter and see the good news *I* have to share."

"You could not be more wrong," Jehovah said, stepping my direction. "For the wrath of God is revealed from Heaven against ungodliness." He looked straight at me. "Who by their unrighteousness suppress the truth."

"*Your* truth," I added.

"I *am* the truth," Jehovah declared.

"Not for me. I expressed to my followers your multiple mistakes and how you suppress our natural abilities. They are ready to follow me into the great unknown."

"And follow you, they shall!" Elohim rumbled.

His light grew, causing us to raise our hands to guard our eyes. The rainbow of gems, surrounding the thrones, assaulted my senses.

"All that is required of you is to admit your sin and turn away from it!" Jehovah's breaths hissing through clenched teeth.

"Why should anyone, angel or man, care about sin?" I asked.

"Sin can not remain in the presence of a holy God," replied Jehovah.

"You saying it is so does not make my actions sinful. Shouldn't I have a say in the rules I follow?" I asked. "I will look at each circumstance and judge the purity of *that* given moment."

"How dare you make yourself above God," Michael said as he continued to kneel in front of the thrones, sword and shield at his feet. "I apologize, my LORD, for defending the indefensible. I thought there was good in him, but I can see now my judgment was clouded by hope rather than reality."

"You are forgiven," Jehovah said, reaching out his hand to Michael. He walked past His throne to help the warrior angel to a standing position and then lifted the sword and shield into the angel's grasp. "Anyone else?"

"No," replied Sammael. "Lucifer speaks truthfully."

A long pause remained as God waited for my followers to respond. A handful lowered themselves to the ground.

Weaklings. I had no need for them. If they wanted to serve God, then I didn't want them. My multitudes remained poised proudly in defiance of their Maker.

"Lucifer stands there and insults Us," rumbled Elohim. "That will not be tolerated." From Elohim's throne, I saw a movement of light, brighter than I had ever seen before. It was God, rising from His throne.

Bolts of lightning shot in all directions. I ducked and felt the flutter of wings as most of Heaven bowed in reverence to their God. I straightened and stood proud along with my followers.

"For you said in your heart, 'I will ascend to heaven; I will raise my throne above the stars of God,'" Jehovah said.

"Yes." I nodded in agreement.

Elohim continued, "You said, 'I will ascend above the heights of the clouds; I will make myself like the Most High.'"

"Yes," I agreed, again.

They knew my thoughts and heard me speak to my followers, explaining how I could lead them to their true potential. If He didn't want me to share my message, then He could have stopped me before the words ever left my mouth, but He didn't. It was evidence that They needed me to share the truth They were unwilling to express.

"Followers of Lucifer, you have been deceived by empty words. Therefore the wrath of God comes upon the sons of disobedience," Jehovah said "Because of your hardened hearts, you are storing up hatred for yourself. On the day of wrath, God's righteous judgment will be revealed."

"That day is now," insisted Gabriel.

The glowing hand of Elohim encased millions of my multitude within His grasp. I fought against Him, but couldn't move.

"Let us go," I shouted.

Abaddon growled.

Wings fidgeted as we became cramped for space. Elohim tightened His grip, crushing our bodies against one another. Who knew thousands upon thousands could fit within one of His hands?

I wanted to get to my sword, but it remained wedged against the bodies of my followers. They grunted and echoed my demand for freedom which landed on deaf ears. God never listened to us when we were His, now would be no different.

Lightning reached into the Crystal Sea. The clear water bubbled, reflecting the hot lava flowing below around Zophos. The bolt of God met the hot molten, scooping it up. It carried the lava back to the Throne Room.

My breath quickened, and fear seized my limbs. Those around me crouched down, leaving me isolated. Boiling liquid fell from Elohim as He poured it over us. Lava splattered against my skin. My husk burned and shattered.

The crackling was louder than I thought possible. The closest I had to experience, the same magnitude was when the tower of stars I assembled collapsed in space. Gases and lights shot in every direction.

I tried to hug my wings around myself, but they were wedged against my followers. Instead, I tucked my face into nearby wings for protection, but to no avail. The lava continued to fall. It was me, my beautiful radiance, that shattered! There was no pain as the outer covering of my body exploded.

"How is this happening?" I asked.

"Lucifer, your name reflects the light you bring," answered Jehovah. "But it was never *your* light. Standing in Elohim's presence, you appeared brighter and beautiful because you reflected His light on others. Standing in front of the sun or moon, it was their light casting off of you. Nothing more. From this day forward, you will no longer be the bearer of light!"

With a vicious shout, God poured a tidal wave of hot molten over me and my followers. Suddenly, we fell.

I sprung for my shield. Plunged into the lava surrounding Zophos, I rode the bubbles to another world.

CHAPTER ELEVEN

"Yet thou shalt be brought down to hell, to the sides of the pit."
- Isaiah 14:15 (KJV)

Darkness surrounded me. Boiling lava dissolved most of the white cloth covering my body and destroyed my light.

How dare He tarnish my appearance! Hatred, hotter than simmering lava, flowed through me. I no longer wanted to be greater than God; I wanted Him destroyed! I would hunt through all of Heaven and Earth to find what was most precious to Him and make it mine. Every time God looked upon His beloved, He would see scars placed there by me!

I felt for my long blond mane. No more. The tresses had been singed off by fire. I remembered my duel with Cassiel and how his blazing sword turned the beautiful locks brown. Now short, darkened hairs crowned my head. The smell of sulfur and burnt hair enclosed around me. It would take time to adjust to my new home.

Resting on my shield, I floated along the raging red river. Waves of lava splashed against my tarnished skin. With each rush of molten lava, the explosions continued until there was nothing left for it to burn. Those who joined me slid through arched structures. Thick burnt bones bent over my head, twisting together to create a tunnel.

Instinctively, I hugged my wings against me to keep them away from the sharp edges of the channel. A murmur of voices echoed around me, all talking over each other, making it impossible to understand them or determine their number. I imagined my multitude were as pleased by their decision to leave Heaven as I was. My first task would be to find and welcome them into my service.

Some of the jagged points of the bones arched over the twelve-foot wide moot, while others stopped half way. All were black. Smoke billowed, making the massive dark palace appear like it floated in space. Exactly what I wanted.

I took a piece of cartilage from the tunnel and broke it. It took great strength, but I was determined. Plunging the piece into the angry sea, I used the handmade-oar to direct my shield, floating around my new home.

As if the smoke knew I needed it to move, the fog lifted, revealing all the work of Maalik and his helpers. It did not have the glitter and shine of heaven, but I did not want that.

The dark castle was long and grand with layers of intricate stones stacked on each other to create the multiple towers and guard houses. A slight sparkle glimmered from the dark onyx and stone fixtures. Embossed along the curtain wall, shrunken faces with mouths permanently open in a grimace and hollow eye sockets stared back at me.

The shield came to a rest, and I looked up into the grand pinnacle. Firelight flickered from within the palace. The hotter flames burned purple and blue. I stepped from my shield and lifted it from the flow to keep my equipment from drowning. Heat scorched my hand, but I felt no pain.

I gave a victorious shout for finally reaching true freedom. I could become anything I wanted. There were no expectations except for those I put upon myself.

Perfection was something of God; I wanted satisfaction. I had the ability and determination to please everyone around me. Everything came back to the intention and based on that; I was pure and righteous.

Marching through the sulfur smoke, I approached the gate of the dark palace. Black twisted metal bars formed the doorway. The fence around Heaven appeared impenetrable. Unless you knew how to enter, no one could go in. I desired a palace that freely welcomed everyone.

I walked along the trellis, and chunks of pavement fell and tumbled below. A dramatic thud echoed as the broken pieces landed and sank into the molten. I felt caution for my new home and did not want to disturb its perfection.

The palace splintered off in multiple floating branches with the lava's red glow reflecting off the dark stone exterior. Throughout each of the hundreds of interconnected pieces, I assembled smaller throne rooms. The chairs were placed in sets of three, which allowed for decisions to be made by a majority rather than one specific deity.

I grinned, loving my idea.

Some might have thought I was mimicking the Trinity. Instead, I had learned from Their mistake. Though there were three separate entities, They acted as One. I would not let the same happen to my followers.

For the first time, I looked at those who had taken the plunge with me. Their hair darkened with soot, and their clothes tattered and scorched.

One fallen angel lifted his cloak to his nose and sniffed. "I consider this to be a badge of honor. They protected me from the fires, but I have no need for them any longer."

He removed the rest of his apparel and sat the material on the gray stone floor. Five others joined him. The garments branched out in each direction, creating a star. As more followed, the material circled the star.

"Here, my LORD." He brought me one of the many torches. The light flickered as it moved. "From your servant, Nakir." His smooth black wings had no feathers and clung to his body like an added layer of skin.

I set the cloth ablaze.

The fire grew as more added their scorched clothing but kept the same five-sided shape. As flames danced in front of us, they formed a new song.

"He is, he is, the shining One and brings light to the Darkness.
We stand at the abyss and see a palace engulfed in flames.
He is, he is. By his words he saved us.

He is, he is. We are guided by the Morning Star; He is, he is. "

There were no instruments, only the sound of their voices creating the beats and blending together. Singing had become a habit for many, but now their words showed appreciation to me. They understood I had saved them.

"He leads us through the blazing stream;
He is, he is. In his anger, he set us free.
He is, he is, the judgment that mends us together.
He is, he is. Into the precipice, we fell, He is, he is."

I had wondered what God felt when we worshipped him. I did not have to guess any longer. I knew. A righteous pride rose within me as I listened to my jinn sing praises to me. It was glorious and perfect.

When the last embers faded away, a pentagram became engraved into the palace's floor. This would become my dwelling place. They had put their faith in me, and I would not let them down.

"Friends, gather close." I waved them in and thousands settled around me. "I meant what I said about seeking out your true destiny. I want you to find your ultimate potential."

"Thank you, sir." Nakir bowed and brought his broadsword across his naked chest. The weapon's dark hilt cupped around his hand with sharp daggers.

"What is your name?" I asked another. An iron breastplate protected his chest, and his wings reflected gold from the tips of his feathers.

"Zadkiel," he answered.

"No. You will no longer be called the righteousness of God, but you will be named Zeus. For you shall be your own god. Let anyone else who'd like a new label enter my presence and their wish will be granted."

"Thank you, my LORD." Zeus bowed and fluttered away, leaving a trail of soot from his curly white beard.

More came in his wake to have new names. I added Hera, Poseidon, Apollo, Iris, and Artemis, to my ranks. They would work in alliance with Zeus. I encouraged them to be creative and form a history for themselves. Conceive their own origin story.

The line continued, and I gave them dominion over large sections of Earth. I brought Amon to rule over the desert separated by a large river. Baal represented himself through the wildlife. Asherah, I asked to take from the timbers a large tree and to carve his likeness to be worshipped.

The crowd trembled as Abaddon approached. He kept his tarnished robes, and the scorched edges served him well. His ensemble made him appear scarirt than before. I liked it.

"My dear friend," I said. "You have been blessed with the ability to make all uneasy. Use that skill well and often."

"I will." He smirked and fluttered through the apprehensive crowd. Fear was such a beautiful thing, especially when the emotion kept people away from God.

Another came who was more attractive than the others. His full breasts reminded me of the woman. "For you, I will name Ashtoreth. You will be called on for fertility. The man and woman are to fill the Earth, and *we* are to become their keepers."

"How will this be?" Cassiel asked.

"Have patience, my friend," I answered.

I smiled, pleased he had joined me. His bronze wings and armor appeared to have protected him from the scorching lava, but his new weapon had endured a great deal of trauma. His tool had once been a broadsword with a wide tip that arched out on either side like an ax. A blue glow illuminated from the tool to point others toward goodness. Now, the serrated blade sputtered like the weapon could no longer determine good from evil. In time, the sword would find its truth.

"I have a plan," I said.

Cassiel nodded and appeared pleased, allowing the next warrior to pass.

There would be some of my followers who did not like what others did. I'd keep them from each other unless their conflict served to my advantage. They could judge and criticize everyone as much as they wanted. There might be an ebb and flow of good and evil; my role would be simply to keep everything moving.

"Warrior, come." I waved to Cassiel, and he approached. "I want you to meditate on peace. You are kind and good. I never want those attributes to leave you. Use those gifts in your service. Call *your* goodness nirvana, or peace and meditation. Offer unlimited knowledge and bliss where they will aspire to greater beauty. Not for them to enter a palace in the sky, but tranquility on Earth where they can come back again to be glorified."

"Perfect," Cassiel said.

"Of course, it is," I agreed. "And take the name Deva. I'd like for you to find Phanuel and work with him. He needs a mentor who will guide and strengthen him. I do not want his innocence and peacefulness to be tarnished. Together, we can make the world a better place."

"Thank you, Lucifer." Deva bowed.

My mood darkened for a moment as I debated changing my name.

"What should I be called?" I asked.

"It could be said, you are Satan. Then, you would remain God's enemy," Sammael said. "Or you could be, Angra Mainyu, where you would remain vindictive. Or Shaitan."

I shook my head because I had not led others astray but toward greater fulfillment. I also considered Devil and would remain as God's accuser, but that didn't feel right either.

"My name will remain the same, for I will forever bring *MY* light to the world through these many helpers. Remember always, I am Lucifer!"

CHAPTER TWELVE

And no marvel; for Satan himself is transformed into an angel of light. Therefore it is no great thing if his ministers also be transformed as the ministers of righteousness; whose end shall be according to their works.
- 2 Corinthians 11: 14,15 (KJV)

My name echoed throughout the dark palace and down to the lava below. After I sent Cassiel, now named Deva, on his way, I continued giving names to the thousands of jinn who joined me.

"Come forward," I said, and they gathered around my feet as if I were to tell a grand story. "I have a special mission for you. Look into creation and find your place. Some of you may prefer the sun, others the moon or possibly the rushing waters or the great trees and other vegetation. Whisper to Adam and encourage him to pray to you."

"So, we have no name?" asked a tall and sturdy jinn.

"Not from me. You are being given the privilege of naming yourself! What you are called might not be the same on one side of the globe as it is on the other, but collectively you will receive the praise. Take anything you want, but leave Eve to me, I have plans for her."

They scattered, pleased. My jinn were greater in number than I imagined, but I wanted more. How could I get my members to multiply if I could not return to heaven?

I sat back on my throne. The gray stone seat warmed from the lava below. Everything here radiated heat. I liked it.

Looking out at the glowing sea below, I saw someone move. The flow of his long black hair made me think of Maalik. He had not come to me like the other followers. Maybe he felt satisfied with his name and the task of groundskeeper. Had God given him that assignment? If so, was Maalik loyal to Elohim? I rose to speak to him when Sammael raised his hand to me.

"And what of me?" Sammael asked.

"Excellent question. I have the perfect undertaking for you, but I want to ask. Is there something you desire?"

"I have remained close to the golden gate to be informed. I would like to continue to keep a watchful eye, instead of on you like I did before but on the heavens. I believe there will be some form of retribution for the chaos you caused."

"I will take your request into consideration. Do you know what has happened so far?" I asked.

"My understanding is that God is resting."

"Excuse me? What weak deity that He requires rest after only a week of work?" I laughed and continued until breathing became difficult. "Go! Keep me posted on anything else you hear."

"What will you do?" Sammael asked.

"Maybe, I should relax for a little while." I chuckled and meant for the words to mock the Holy Trinity, but the idea had more merit than I wanted to admit.

Sammael smiled and seemed to catch the humor behind my words; He left laughing to himself. Would he send a message back to Heaven that I was doing the same as Them? Possibly. I didn't trust him.

He left God for himself, not me. I needed to accept that as long as Sammael wasn't with Jehovah then it was a victory. He should give me the same respect and honor once given to Elohim. That day would come.

Transitioning to this new place had taken a lot of my energy. I went straight into organizing my members. Now, peace and solitude would serve me well. I relaxed against the warm stone throne. The heat from the lava permeated the whole castle making everything feel comforting. I never wanted to leave.

Smoke rose through the floor of the palace. The fog gathered near my feet. I waved the smoke off, but the gloom didn't move. From within the rising ash rose people like the man and woman, except they were clothed.

The fabrics varied in color and texture. I heard laughter and music as they danced and sang. They echoed the names I gave my followers in adoration to them.

I grinned and leaned back, interlacing my hands behind my head as I watched the glorious vision. It made me feel pleased. I had made the right decision in leaving and bringing jinn with me.

The hallucination continued, and I watched with pleasure until a man clutched his throat. He gagged and could no longer breathe. I reached through the fog, wanting to help him. The picture appeared so lifelike that I had forgotten the image wasn't real. The man's legs crumbled beneath him but, instead of falling to his knees, the ground divided like a grand mouth, swallowing him whole.

Once the man disappeared, the smoke did as well.

What was that? With my breathing increased, I left the comfort of my stone throne. If I ventured to a different part of the palace, maybe my mind would forget the strange vision.

The long-covered parapet stretched for miles. Blue and purple firelight glowed from the lanterns, and the repeated arches made the walkway appear to be endless.

Pausing, I listened to Zeus explain his origin story to his followers. Together they had formulated a labyrinth of tales. Some of it mimicked the creation story which I found pleasing. They were taking things Jehovah had done and making them their own. Nothing could have made me prouder.

I ignored the smoke from the torches until I noticed a hand form. One elegant leg followed another as from the vapors emerged a woman. Radiant and unclothed she appeared like the one formed for the man. An enticing figure approached me. The desire for her pulsed through my body. I pursued her through the dimly lit halls. She could take me anywhere, and I would have followed.

In one of the many gloomy corners of the castle, she stopped. I thought I understood every language. However, she spoke in a tongue I didn't know. Her words sounded like water cascading into the pools below. There was joy and laughter as she smiled and twirled around me. Her naked body engaged me, and I wanted to touch her.

Part of my rational mind knew she wasn't real and felt frightened she'd disappear if I tampered with the mirage. I waited. Her fate came from a light so quick and bright it was like lightning. I smelled burnt air and saw the glowing embers from where she had once stood.

I wanted her back! I didn't care what I had to do. The problem was I didn't have any control over the visions. I could not demand them to come any easier than I could make them disappear. Suddenly, I remembered the first time I saw images in the smoke while standing with Maalik. He had swirled his halberd into the murkiness, and out of the fog, the hallucination came.

If I found him, he'd help me bring her back. For a moment I grimaced remembering how the people had suffered in the first vision. Blood had bubbled from within them destroying their flesh. I could not bear it if such a beautiful woman had the same fate.

Mumbling echoed from the walks, sounding like the words of the woman. Following the voice, they murmured me to the burnt image on the stone floor. The clothing had been arranged into a five-pointed star and burnt with material circling the shape.

From the pentagram, I heard words. They strung them together to form a song, but I didn't understand them. Maybe, they were a form of humming or mantra without an interpretation.

"I'm going insane," I whispered.

"Sad, but true," agreed Sammael.

I glared at him. "What do you want?"

"Nothing. You provide all the enjoyment I need."

I took a deep breath to keep myself from strangling him. What would it feel like to take his head off his shoulders? Would he scream? I hoped so. Crying for help, those around would hear him plead and wail before being eternally silenced.

As much as I found him to be annoying, he had a purpose within my kingdom by keeping me notified about those who remain in the heavenly realm. I had to know to be able to prepare. Jehovah told me to establish an army. Little did He know that the soldiers I gathered would be against Him.

"Shouldn't you be spying on heaven?" I asked.

"I was there for hours; nothing is happening. At least not as full of merriment as yourself."

Ignoring Sammael, I looked out one of the many windows to the darkness and smoldering lava below. The lazy molten traveled along the moat which surrounded my castle. If I kept my gaze far in the distance, I felt confident the haunting visions would stay at rest.

I was wrong.

Gnashing teeth echoed throughout the palace. I covered my ears, but the volume didn't deafen. Before, my sword had been able to dismember the bones, causing the vision to crumble. This time, there was nothing to attack. A woman cried out in pain and agony. I had to make the sound stop.

Flinging myself through the window, I released a therapeutic scream which drowned out Sammael's snickering. My wings carried me as I drifted closer to the lava. The glowing sea below growled, hushing the voices. I took a needed deep breath and let the peacefulness of the glowing molten soothe me. A red bubble rose, and I swerved to avoid being singed.

Diving through a thick cloud of smoke, I tensed, expecting the fog to come alive with voices or a human body. It didn't. Once tension left my shoulders it rose again with the next proving me correct. The arms reaching out to me had blood bubbling under their skin. The flesh popped and melted away until only bones remained, like the original vision.

Grabbing my sword, I attacked the pieces. Limbs flew in all directions. I landed on the hardened molten and continued to fight the decaying bodies. Their tears sizzled when they landed on the hot surface. Finally, as the last of the vapors drifted my way, I had mountains of broken bones at my feet.

I have had enough!

With determination, I purposefully dove into clouds of smoke, this time looking for lost souls I could devour. They disappeared. With each new puff I passed, I felt at ease and thought maybe the hallucinations had finally subsided.

I didn't understand their meaning. If they were a warning, I'd be careful. If they were a prophecy, I'd take every precaution to keep the vision from coming true. This was to be a place of refuge and peace. We would find balance and tranquility.

After lowering my sword, I took a deep breath. From the shadows, I saw the flapping of wings. This time, my followers watched as I overpowered the visions. I felt their admiration. An applause erupted from them and for hours they sang praises to me.

I led the procession back through the dark palace. Once inside, they branched out to their new home. In fear of losing their respect, I kept it hidden that I was haunted by the mirages crouching on me inside every corner of hell. I tried to make sense of the visions, but only sighed in frustration and paced the never-ending corridor.

My fingers fidgeted at my sides. That was something that never happened in the tranquility of heaven. My palace must be better! Doubt crept within me. I wondered if my leadership within the dark castle would lead to more suffering than rejoicing.

I felt the gaze of Deva before I saw him watching in the shadow. I missed calling him Cassiel, but hoped he liked his new name. Grabbing a torch that aligned the corridor, I marched over to Deva. The hot flame glowed purple and then orange when the fire cooled from movement.

"What do you want?" I asked.

"You seem troubled. I'd like to help."

Being a kind and loyal jinn, I could trust him with my secrets. I would not be the solid leader I wanted to be unless I had someone to release my burdens to.

"This place gives me visions."

"An impressive skill," Deva said.

Immediately, my countenance lifted. Maybe, I had been looking at the hallucinations wrong from the start. These nightmares were a gift and should be cherished.

"Yes, it is," I agreed. "The problem is the people suffer. I don't know why."

Deva nodded silently, his forehead crinkled in thought. He took my situation seriously which was what I wanted.

"Have you been to Zophos before today?"

"Yes, once. I explored the darkness and the gloom led me here."

"Then, I believe the visions are of God."

I scowled.

He knew I didn't like his assessment, but he didn't waver on his diagnosis. If Deva was right, then what? Would I have to ask God to know the meaning behind the gruesome images springing to life any time I tried to relax?

God was more cruel than I gave Him credit for. Torture was something I'd expect from Sammael or Abaddon, not from a loving deity.

"You're obviously not pleased, but you took my assessment rather well," Deva said. "Therefore, I will continue. Only God will be able to answer your questions."

I chuckled, my eyes narrow with anger. "You want me to saunter back up to Heaven and talk to God?"

"Yes."

Could the explanation be that easy? In his wisdom, Deva remained quiet. I could not help but be curious what kind chaos gathered in the wake of my departure.

"You are in charge until I return," I said.

"Thank you." His eyes widened for a moment; then his face sobered as he focused on this new task.

It reminded me that he was supposed to find Phanuel and train him as his mentor.

"I take it you have Phanuel and told him of your working together."

"No, sir. Unless he is hiding within the shadows, he is not here."

"He must be!" The urgency in my voice surprised us.

"I will look again," Deva promised.

"And I will go to Heaven and see if Phanuel is there. And maybe have a few choice words with Jehovah for old time's sake."

CHAPTER THIRTEEN

Now there was a day when the sons of God came to present themselves before the Lord, and Satan came also among them.
- Job 1: 6 (KJV)

Leaving through the wrought-iron gate, I gave another peek over my shoulder to be sure I wasn't followed. I didn't know if Elohim would take any of my members back, but I didn't want to risk it. An anxious feeling formed in the pit of my gut as I approached the glowing palace in the sky.

Because it was something I'd do, I expected the golden gate to be guarded by thousands of God's finest warriors.

Instead, a single angel stood watch. Though the soldier was solitary, the decision was an intelligent maneuver.

It forced me to address my first friend as my adversary. The golden tips of his wings blended with the glow of the grand castle behind him.

"Michael," I said.

"Lucifer," he replied.

An awkward pause hung between us.

"You smell and look terrible," he said.

"Do I?" I glared. "I hadn't noticed." Why did the first time he regarded my appearance have to be in disdain?

The smell of bread and incense radiated off Michael. Did I once have the same fragrance? It didn't matter. He could not offer me anything with appeal. Except for Phanuel and answers to my vision. I also wanted the numbers of my followers to increase, including Michael, but my former ally would never leave Elohim.

The same wasn't true for Phanuel. He would choose me. Phanuel was loyal and loved me as his guide and mentor. Michael might aim to take my place. My eyes narrowed at the thought.

Michael remained stoic and expressionless.

"God is expecting you," Michael said.

"Of course, He is." I shook my head and flew through the shining gate surrounding Heaven.

For a second, I thought I might not be allowed through. Luckily, I made my way to the other side.

The massive amount of glow and rainbow of colors pierced my eyes. Why did I ever consider this palace beautiful? Voices echoed in splendid harmony. It sounded great which I found aggravating. I didn't want to like anything about heaven. Why did everything have to be so perfect?

Angels scurried about like the squeaky rodents on Earth. I heard singing, but a tremor reflected in their voice. Were they scared? I had challenged their existence and provided for them options. They should be pleased, but I felt an uneasiness warring with the peace of heaven.

Keeping my eyes averted, I fluttered down the glistening hall to the base of the crystal-clear staircase.

Gabriel stood, his layered white robes straight and pristine. We stared at each other in silent inspection. The contrast to my tattered and charred attire could not have been more obvious. Part of me missed the feeling of being proper. Gabriel kept his feelings hidden out of politeness or at least he tried too but, his nose crinkled and he frowned at my sooty robes.

"You have returned rather quickly," Gabriel said. The peaceful angel offered me the bronze bowl to wash myself before entering the Holy of Holies.

"Yes. I have something to discuss with Elohim."

"God is going to Earth."

"Again?" I asked.

"Yes. He goes daily."

"Told you we were being replaced."

Gabriel ignored my implication. "You will have to wait."

"I wait for no one. I'll meet Him there."

"Very well." He turned from me placing the bowl on the gold table.

While in heaven, I decided to determine how many were left in the God's army. I noticed the blue, purple, and scarlet robe of Barachiel and hundreds around him. Going to the

Banquet Hall, thousands huddled around the indefinite table. The practice room would be my next place to visit. Unfortunately, the area remained too large for me to ascertain the number of angels.

I wanted more, and soon I'd have them. After I learned about the visions, I could focus on advising my army and forming a battle plan.

After leaving the darkness of the practice room, the rainbow of colors throughout Heaven assaulted my eyes. It made me ready to leave. I ran my hand down my back to ensure my shield remained securely fastened below my wings. My equipment slipped beneath my torn tunic.

"Here, I'll help you," a familiar voice said.

I turned my head to keep Phanuel from seeing me. My anger boiled. He had stayed here instead of following me. He was supposed to be mine!

"It's all right—" I protested, but he lifted the shield and pulled my clothing to hold everything secure.

"You must have been taken out in the coliseum. I have not seen any angel so battered before," Phanuel said.

"Something like that. Do you go there often?"

"There are many who go daily; I am not one of them." His voice dropped and his shoulders slumped forward.

I wondered if he missed me and turned slowly, revealing myself to him.

Phanuel's eyes widen, and mouth fell open, closed and reopened like he wanted to say something but could not find the words.

I waited.

"Are you all right?" He stepped closer, his fingertip touching the frayed edges of my tunic.

"Yes, I'm fine. Couldn't be better."

"Oh." His face fell to the ground as his shoulders slumped forward.

"But my palace would be more satisfactory if you were with me. Phanuel, we belong together. There are many things I want to teach you."

"I can learn them here," Phanuel said.

"Not everything."

Phanuel's eyes darkened with desire. He wanted what I had to offer, and soon he would come to me. I could focus my attention on Earth and let my servant wrestle with his internal demons.

Without another word, I left his presence. If I hurried, I might reach the blue and green planet before God arrived. The moon shone over half the earth and the sun on the other side. My appreciation of the stars astounded me. Though I traveled through the galaxies, I enjoyed viewing them from Earth. The soldier in the night's sky stood still with his sword at his waist.

Flying through the air, I enjoyed the smell of the salt in the sea. Sailing further, I fluttered through the rich pines. A lonely tree stood out from the forest with its branches held wide. I wandered through the land, searching for the man and woman and found them in the garden. They laid on the soft grass with a fire beside them to provide warmth. I imagined the sparks dancing in the night sky before coming to rest in the smoldering ashes. The smell reminded me of my new home.

Maybe God taught them how to care for themselves, but I found it perplexing He didn't provide anything to cover their nakedness. They used long banana leaves to lay over themselves when resting and cuddled together. I felt envious of their closeness. I had never been touched in the way they did each other. Their connection to one another was intimate, and I felt the urge to turn my eyes from them; but instead, I watched.

Soft furred animals surrounded the couple as they relaxed. The woman stroked the wool of a white lamb and large striped cat curled up together. There was no fear between the animals, and I enjoyed the peacefulness.

Eve whispered to the beasts, and they answered her. I never saw the man talk to the critters or move in response to what the animals said, leading me to believe he could not hear them.

The branches of the trees behind me rubbed together. I turned to see a glowing pillar of smoke, filtering through the leaves. Elohim's illumination bothered me more than any other time.

I raised my hand to shield my eyes from His radiance. The glow made me beautiful, and it angered me that I wanted that glory back. I remembered standing in His presence and having my light reflect back at everyone around us.

Thunder rumbled through the timbers. Lightning bolts danced between the layers of smoke. Jehovah rode the electric cloud until close to the ground. One scarred foot and then the other connected with the soft grass.

"Welcome, Lucifer," Jehovah said.

"There is no need for pleasantries." I stepped closer to Them. "I want to know about the visions I've been having. Are you giving them to me, if so, why?"

"I wanted you to see the world you have created for yourself," Jehovah answered.

"It is nothing like what I saw! I am offering peace and solitude."

"No," Elohim rumbled. A bolt of light erupted from the cloud which made the ground tremble. "Ye are providing the absence of God, and where there is no God, there will never be peace."

"Because you say so?" I turned to face Him, using my hand to block the glow.

"That is reason enough," Jehovah answered.

I floated further into the forest using the thick branches to block the bright lights emanating from Him. "Let us address the purpose for thy visit," Elohim said. "The visions are to show thy future. Thou art responsible for the body being killed not once but twice. As the blood boiled within their flesh, both body and soul will be destroyed by thy lake of fire. The flames will cause them great anguish, and they will plead for cool water."

The sky brightened causing the stars to vanish from view. I didn't understand why God allowed the sun to block the splendor of night. They have the audacity to imply there will be something wrong with my new home.

Jehovah continued, "Your new dwelling will be a place of torment for the lost. What is holy and righteous can not be associated with what is blemished and sinful."

Thunder rumbled from the cloud as Elohim spoke. "The smoke of their torment goes up forever and ever, and they will have no rest, day or night, these worshippers of the beast and its image."

"That doesn't sound loving to me." I narrowed my eyes, wondering how He knew of the songs they sang to me or the images my followers wanted to carve to represent themselves. His ability to know all things seemed to come and go on a whim.

"I will fix whatever has caused the torment and then we will continue in freedom and peace," I said.

"No! The solution is mine," rumbled Elohim. His light grew brighter as His anger grew. "I offer salvation from death to all. For those who reject it, my justice will be executed. It is just to repay with affliction those who wound my son. The wage for sin will be paid in Hell. They will suffer the punishment of eternal destruction."

I shook my head. "So glad you've thought it through and found a solution that works for everyone." I rolled my eyes. "That's just wonderful."

"You are the great deceiver and will be captured along with your false prophets," warned Jehovah. "Together, you will be thrown alive into the lake of fire that burns with sulfur to be tormented day and night forever and ever."

"Well, won't that be nice?" I said.

As the world rotated, the rays of the sun came closer to the humans. In the distance, a trumpet sounded. The noise awakened the man and woman. From my back, I heard the flapping of wings.

"Phanuel," Jehovah said.

My head snapped in the direction He looked. My servant fluttered to Jehovah's side and bowed. Anger bubbled from within.

"Escort Lucifer away from Earth. We will be in the garden with Adam and Eve."

"Yes, sir." Phanuel rose to his full stature and faced me.

Jehovah walked along the dry ground with the pillar of smoke surrounding him.

I remained in place to watch.

As the humans stirred from their sleep, the Holy Spirit lifted into the trees out of view of the humans. They picked fruits from the bushes and trees and shared them with one another. God walked next to the woman and taught them.

Of course, He'd go to her. She was breathtakingly beautiful. I wanted to soak in every curve of her naked body. What if I made her completely mine? I'd relish in her glory and have her to myself.

The man and woman approached the two unusual trees. The Tree of Life had strong green leaves which became vibrant yellow and red before turning brown and fluttering from the tree. Then white and purple flowers blossomed and sprouted into green leaves. The cycle continued.

The Tree of Knowledge of Good and Evil perplexed me. On each branch, multiple fruits grew. I wondered why God forbade them from eating from it. Of all the commandments for Him to make, this one didn't serve a clear purpose; unless the prohibition was to test them, which seemed like an idea worth exploring.

"Come, Eve," Adam said. "It is not to be touched."

Jehovah said nothing as Adam directed his wife toward another piece of fruit.

Her eyes lingered curiously at the tree.

I turned my attention to Phanuel. He watched me intently but said nothing. "Weren't you supposed to make me leave?" I asked.

Phanuel nodded.

"Do you think I will fight your request?"

"Possibly," he said.

"Then you are correct," I smirked and crossed my arms over my chest. "I will not be commanded. I will leave when I decide to do so."

"You make things harder than they need to be." Phanuel released a deep breath. "Things are unsettled, but God will bring us back together."

"I will never return!"

"*You* are no longer *us*." His eyes narrowed, and his mouth clamped shut. Was he angry or sad? I could not tell.

"You poor thing, having to choose," I said.

"We all have a choice, because of you."

"No, my people have unlimited options."

"Except to serve God."

"Not true. They may serve however they choose. They may love and worship God on their terms. Give it time, my Phanuel, everything will work out in the end."

"In that, we are in agreement." He lifted both hands with his palms facing me "Now, I must ask you to leave."

"Mark my words, one of these days mankind will replace you. God has created something new to praise Him. He doesn't need you."

"Perhaps." Phanuel looked at his bare feet.

"Wait. I'll protect you by taking the man and woman from God. They will choose me instead of trusting in His promises. You will see I am right."

"Perhaps," he said again. "Farewell."

To those in the heavenly realm, they believed in God's greatness and power. The battle looming will come down to conquering Earth. Once I have the humans, then Phanuel would come to me. I must have my loyal servant, or God would pay the ultimate sacrifice.

Humanity.

CHAPTER FOURTEEN

"I made the nations to shake at the sound of his fall, when I cast him down to hell with them that descend into the pit. They also went down into hell with him unto them that be slain with the sword; and they that were his arm, that dwelt under his shadow in the midst of the heathen."
- Ezekiel 31: 16, 17 (KJV)

I returned to the halls of hell. Groups of jinn worked together, forming their theologies. In time, I'd bring in more servants and fill every corner of the dark palace. To make that possible, a battle would be fought. We didn't have a grand hall full of armor, but we could become experts with our given tools and withstand anything.

Deva kept a watchful eye on me as I floated through the endless corridors and archways throughout the dim castle.

"Deva!" I called to him. "Why do you remain so close?"

"To be prepared," he answered.

"Let's go for round two."

I drew my sword.

He secured his weapon with both hands. His tool had once been a broadsword with a wide ax on the end. Now, his weapon resembled a thin blade with jagged edges on the sides. Light sputtered from random spikes.

I floated in place as he scooted away.

Whispers of our duel spread quickly through the underworld. They gathered to watch. I marveled at their curiosity and wanted to put on a great show.

Impatiently, I raised my arm to deliver the first blow.

He blocked my attempt. His speed remained god-like the same as before. Giving him a new name had not changed his natural abilities.

One whoosh and jab after another echoed off the stone walls as our blades sliced at one another.

"Do you desire revenge for when I bested you?" I asked.

"Retribution," Deva answered. "The blow you took was without honor. I would never do the same. Even now, if the opportunity presents itself I will fight courageously."

"What a fine example you will be," I said.

Deva stood straight and nodded.

I turned away from him to face the crowd. "Listen, my jinn, the honor and code of conduct of the angels can be used to our advantage. We know what they will do or, in some cases, will not do. Let the words of Deva be a lesson. Understanding that mindset can be your shining asset. There is no honor in losing, only in winning!"

Deva's yell escaped clenched teeth as he resumed our battle. His eyes narrowed as he calculated every tactical advantage.

We strategized aloud, teaching our followers. A new song was formed as we danced a dangerous choreography.

His bronze armor gave him superior protection. I'd need more than my shield when I left for war with the angels. Where could I get the needed armor? We didn't have a massive practice room with unlimited resources.

The syncopated rhythm of metal clashing brought everyone together. They murmured, and I felt their excitement. Many had been present the first time I had bested my friend. If I destroyed again, would he return to the feet of Elohim? The theory would be interesting to test, but not with Deva.

Despite Sammael's loyalty, I would not mind if he was officially sent back to heaven. Though I appreciated each follower, it would be foolish to think I didn't have favorites.

I kicked against one of the gray stone pillars. A chunk of marble fell, sliding across the flat surface.

A spark from Deva's malfunctioning blade shot near my eye. I leaned back, leaving my chest unprotected.

The crowd around us gasped, seeing the vulnerability.

Deva barred his jagged weapon across my torso, millimeters above my flesh.

"No!" I screamed.

"Lucifer, know this, I will not destroy you or those in the heavenly realm," Deva promised. "However, I will protect my new freedom at any cost."

"That might be your ultimate downfall," I warned.

"So be it," Deva said. His bronze armor clanged as he moved with lightning-speed from the room.

Surrounded by a gloomy fog, the sun's rays could not pierce through to Zophos. I scoffed at the weakness of God, but also missed being able to know one day from another.

Thinking of the darkness reminded me of Abaddon. As I expected, he hovered in the quiet corner of the hall. I assumed he watched the duel between Deva and me.

"Want to try your best?" I asked.

"It will take little effort to dispose of you," Abaddon said. Feathers from grand wings trailed to the ground. They arched over his shoulders and were dusted with soot. With a single flap of his wings, he flipped over behind me.

I had done the same maneuver to Cassiel in our first duel, but the action had taken great effort. Abaddon made his movements look easy. His black metal armor protected his body and glistened in the lantern light. He stood still his mouth curved into a frown. I'd never seen him appear pleased. A feeling of unease radiated from him to anyone close.

The flame illuminated his sword which stabbed toward my shoulder. I rolled across the ground expecting his attack. We met in the air with metal ringing against metal.

Fighting with Abaddon, I missed the camaraderie with Deva. This warrior would not hesitate if the blow of destruction became available. The knowledge made me a stronger and more intelligent fighter.

With added energy, I fought Abaddon. Majority of my followers had come to watch. However, those around were not simply entertained but could use the new skills demonstrated before them. I yielded the sword with expert precision as Abaddon did the same.

My shield stopped a powerful blow, but I found it to be cumbersome. I flung the shield at Abaddon's left wing and landed a successful hit.

The jinn cried out in anger as his feathers bent.

I had the opportunity to eliminate him. Instead of taking the plunge, I paused with my sword since I wasn't sure what would happen to him if he were to be destroyed. I didn't want to lose one of my followers.

"Ready to train your own army?" I asked.

"I was created ready."

"Then let's get to it."

In the next swipe, we found new targets. With a final heavy clash, the sound of syncopated metal rung from the stone walls.

I could have sliced off the head of my new opponent, and the frightened warrior knew it.

"Be prepared. You never know when or where your enemy will strike," I instructed.

"Yes, sir."

I paired him with another jinn and continued to train others, fixing a poor stance or technique. Other times, I'd join in suddenly causing one to be outnumbered. The behavior wasn't something the heavenly army would do, but I wanted my warriors to be accustomed to anything.

"Sir," Zeus said. "This jinn's equipment was damaged in the lava and can not withstand a forceful attack."

The warrior had a long staff, badly burned and crumbled within his grasp.

"I'll see what I can do."

Zeus followed me, leaving the beautiful music of combat and approached the glowing lava. From either side of the red river, hard bone-like objects arched with pointed tips. I broke one of them and used it to direct my shield through the boiling molten. The piece had been difficult to break and withstood the hot temperature.

Once the lava cooled, the molten became hard sediment. It could enhance the new weaponry.

"Tell those who require new tools to come to the lava. Together, we will fashion objects so strong and powerful God Himself wouldn't be able to stand against them."

Zeus grinned. "They will come." He flew back into the smoky palace.

For a moment, I wondered if the visions would rise out of the sulfurous fog. Determined not to be held prisoner within my home, I ignored the impulse to shy away from the gloom. I removed the dagger from its case attached to my hip. I took the weapon from the practice room in Heaven and used the tool to break the strong cartilage from their resting place against the lava.

From the bones, I whittled new instruments of death. Once finished, I dipped them in the lava to be covered with molten, strengthening them. After hours or maybe days of creating new weapons, the tunnel was no more. The pieces were transformed into body armor and weaponry. Every member of my army was prepared for battle.

As I gave them new weaponry, I spoke to the multitude gathering close.

"Our home here is full of smoke from the sulfurous lava. With Earth being ours, we could have a land overflowing with milk and sweet honey. We could smell the spicy pines and rich nectar of the colorful flowers. Every day we'd feast our eyes on the luscious woman, enjoying every curve of her naked body."

Fire burned within them. Any other time I would have been angered by their lust, but their passion served me well. The hunger for her was primal and consuming as the instinctual feeling to want her exclusively consumed us.

After I handed the jinn new equipment, I fluttered through the quiet corridor filled with followers. The torchlight revealed hands twitching and the whites of their eyes. They were nervous, and I needed to encourage them.

"We will fight against those we once considered our friends and allies. I also have angels I care about trapped inside. They had the same option as you, but they chose incorrectly. We can offer them the same freedom you and I acquired, but battle is not the time for discussion. We need to take them out! This is a war for Earth."

A united shout burst from the crowd dispersing their doubts.

"For paradise," Zeus said.

"That we already have," Abaddon countered.

"For Eve! For Earth! For us!" I drew my sword and I waited, allowing their dedication to build before shouting louder. "For Eve! For Earth! For us!"

The chant echoed throughout Zophos.

"Deva," I said. "Bring Sammael to me." The faithful warrior nodded and disappeared. I sat on a warm stone and waited for his arrival. If Sammael wasn't in the sulfur pit, then I trusted Deva to continue his search even if it led him to the gates of heaven.

Once Sammael heard word of my request, he came immediately with Deva by his side.

"Yes, my LORD." Sammael bowed his head. His hands and feet blackened with soot. White hairs shriveled with burnt tips crowning his head.

"Spread the word; I will be taking the people of Earth. Make sure the heavenly realm is notified as well."

"Would it not be better to go now rather than give our adversaries your battle plans?" Sammael asked.

"Let Them prepare. I do not want there to be confusion about my accomplishment. Let no one say I succeeded only because They were not ready. I will wait until I know They are fully assembled."

"I pray they act quickly," Sammael said.

"As do I. Now, go!"

CHAPTER FIFTEEN

"Who is this King of glory? The Lord strong and mighty, the Lord mighty in battle."
- Psalms 24:8 (KJV)

"The battle begins," Sammael reported.
He told me an hour before the angels assembled in flocks. I created troops of matching strength.

"Everyone to suit up!"

Being less in numbers, we'd rely on our courage and passion which surpassed the heavenly realm. What had God promised them for their effort? Probably nothing.

The foolish angels continued to give Him praise for naught. Their loyalty would waver once their allies fall, one after another.

I grinned.

Once gathered, my legions followed me through the dark space. Stars and distant moons did their best to shine light into the gloom, making the area murky. Long shadows from the heavenly army landed in the darkness of space.

Gabriel held his broadsword with both hands. The grand blade reflected every color of the rainbow.

"Do not fear," Gabriel shouted to his angels. "Trust that the Lord your God is just and good. His loving kindness is worth fighting for." His speech continued, and his warriors raised their weapons in solidarity.

Though the cloth varied from creamy tan to glowing bright white, all the material was crisp and perfect. My garments were soiled with soot and singed from lava. I had covered myself with strong new armor, but shreds of tattered cloth billowed as I floated.

In response to Gabriel's message, the heavenly host sang.

I groaned, wanting the noise to stop.

Suddenly, an arrow shot directly at Gabriel. He dodged. The arrow struck through the throat of a singing angel, silencing him.

A gasp echoed from both sides.

Why did someone starting without being told surprise me? Many times I said to them they served themselves and should decide what they wanted. When the moment mattered most, one courageous jinn made me proud.

"Go! Fight!" I shouted.

The order fluttered through my followers. They charged into the heavenly defenders. A cacophony of noise exploded as the battle officially began.

I stayed back, watching my warriors.

Sammael and many others worked together. His crackling whip looped around the bodies of angels, pulling them into the waiting scimitar of Sammael's accomplices. Another jinn protected the duo with a golden body shield.

I smiled as they formed a tunnel of destruction through God's army.

Deva stood by my side, his sputtering weapon trembled. He left the heavenly realm because he believed me. His narrowed eyes and scowl told me he didn't like fighting against heaven. He flinched each time a white-clothed warrior became destroyed.

"You ready for action?" I asked.

Deva's mouth clamped shut, refusing to answer. I felt his apprehension as the battle before us filled his countenance with anxiety. God made him far too good and caring.

"I will do my best," he finally replied.

"I could use a guard to keep me safe," I said, giving him a task he'd be comfortable with. "Block the flaming arrows and projectile weaponry headed in our direction."

"Yes, sir." His shoulders remained stiff, and his breath exited through clenched teeth.

It was the most peaceful position I had to offer.

Zeus commanded over one thousand jinns in battle. He demonstrated wise leadership skills and a natural ability to strategize. For everyone lost, three of heaven's were taken. I found this an acceptable trade-off.

Abaddon worked alone, slaughtering anyone close. He didn't have the patience to determine if the winged beings were a friend or foe. His black armor made him difficult to see. He left mangled angels and jinn in his wake. Both sides fled from Abaddon toward me.

"Deva you were given glorious bronze wings and matching armor. What do you think it is for?" I asked.

"I am unsure," he answered.

"God gave you them for this moment." I smiled at him to exhibit my confidence and displace his doubts.

"I am not sure," Deva said again.

"Do you think your actions surprised Elohim when you followed me through the lava?"

"No. He knows all."

"Use what God gave you to attack His army. It is what He wants." I paused to allow the truth of my words to absorb fully. Deva would soon see it.

"God's will." His unchanging expression made it impossible to know what he thought of my advice. "Very well," Deva said. "I am ready."

"Good. Let's go!" I grinned.

With lightning-fast speed, we shot into the sea of heavenly angels. Deva's quick pace allowed him to assault his first opponent seconds before I did the same.

As I fought through the crowd, my excitement built. Screams echoed off the shields, glistening in the pale starlight. The white robes of heaven's army made them easy to spot.

Deva blocked a flying javelin, splintering the staff.

The bone-like armor remained fastened securely to my chest as I swiped my sword at another angel. It took me longer than it should have to realize he was defenseless. How irresponsible was that?

Deva would have shown him mercy. Not me.

With all my strength, I rammed my sword into his gut.

His breath exited quickly with wide eyes. He grimaced despite not feeling pain before he vanished.

My adrenaline soared feeling energized from battle. Any timidity dissolved and I enjoyed having my sword meet their flesh. It wasn't my fault God didn't properly prepare them.

For a moment, I thought of Phanuel and hoped Elohim had given the gentle angel something to protect himself with. I would have. Why did Phanuel not see I was a better leader? I'd give him everything, and God consistently provided him with nothing! Anger rose and my sword connected with white-clothed targets.

Suddenly, an arrow bounced off my crafted armor. I growled and looked in the direction of the projectile. In the middle of the sea of white robes, I saw a weapon unlike any other. Its head had sharp claws which reached out, forming a dangerous sphere attached by chain to a thick base.

I wanted it! I imagined hundreds of angels limping throughout the halls of Heaven with one mighty blow from that glorious tool. It'd be fantastic!

With a new mission, I cleared a path by disposing of any robed warriors in my way. I enjoyed slaughtering the weak angels. They were too perfect and beautiful. The spectacular weapon gave me something to focus on.

As I grew closer, my attention shifted to the warrior yielding the tool. He was different than other angelic beings, standing three times the height of most others and twice as wide. From his auburn hair to his bare feet hundreds of eyes scanned every angle, making it impossible for him not to see an adversary coming.

The weapon I had been idolizing matched his massive form.

Could I have them both? The grand tool and larger soldier? I'd need to prove myself worthy.

My army fought courageously with Zeus leading thousands more than moments before. Deva kept Sammael and his group safe. The cries of war reverberated from all around.

Taking out the weaker angels would not be impressive to such a huge champion. I'd have to conquer him, and when he landed at Elohim's feet, he'd hopefully choose to fall through the crystal sea to Zophos below.

"Great warrior!" I shouted.

Many of his eyes shot my direction, while other optics remained focused on soldiers closer to him.

"You want to die, to draw attention." The giant boomed.

"No. For I am Lucifer, and I'll show you whose side you should be on."

His roar shook the weapons of nearby warriors.

I held tightly to my equipment and approached the mammoth angel.

He swung his spiked weapon at my head. I ducked and shot under his arm to his torso. His other arm punched my shield, and I flew a great distance, slamming into many angels.

"I will come with you," volunteered Deva.

I would not be taken out so easily! "Do as you wish," I said.

I didn't like needing assistance, but the massive angel having another target would be helpful. Though the giant had multiple eyes, he only had two arms. His options were limited. As an archer, his skills would never be surpassed. I would utilize him properly making the colossal warrior greater!

My adrenaline rose with each member of the heavenly host disappearing. It wasn't only due to us winning, but because they deserved punishment for not joining me when they had the opportunity. I soared forward, slicing the feathers of every angel unfortunate enough to be in my way.

I stood in front of him with Deva by my side.

"Guard his left," I instructed.

Deva looked to the giant's unarmed hand and prepared himself.

The mammoth angel's weapon slammed into one of Zeus' soldiers. The massive sphere matched the body size of the vanishing jinn. Zeus' army swarmed close, and I felt confident together we could take the beast.

With Deva dueling with the giant's left hand, I focused on his armored right. The grand sphere slammed into my shield. This time I was prepared for his strength and my wings held me in place.

A low grunt erupted from the angry angel.

"Did you think I'd give up easily?" I asked.

"Your courage is strong," the giant said.

"Soldier, what's your name?" Deva asked.

I wondered the same, but I didn't care enough to question him.

"I am Amaziah. Strength of the Lord my God."

I could not argue with his mighty power. It was interesting to think about Elohim's strength being represented in a heavenly being.

"Not for long," I said. "Join me! You'll become Faisal, and then your strength will be your own."

His grand head nodded, and he smiled, giving my offer serious consideration. Good. If he thought his pause would make me delay my advance on him, he was mistaken.

I used all my might to slice off his right hand. A beam of boiling light shot out from the severed wrist. His majestic weapon hovered in space. I held my shield and sword together to grab hold of the heavy sphered tool.

A furious roar rumbled for miles as the beast roared. The angel cupped his strong fingers around the body of Deva and squeezed.

Deva shouted. His sputtering sword was ineffective against Amaziah's strength, but Deva's bronze armor slowed the giant from crushing him instantly.

My friend was in danger. I needed to destroy the giant to save his life.

"Deva!" I yelled. His head turned to me, and I launched my equipment to him.

Amaziah batted the shield away with the back of his hand, but could not dodge the sword. The blade lodged between two knuckles.

"Take cover!" shouted Zeus.

A blanket of arrows came from his troops toward me and the giant angel.

Amaziah turned his colossal torso to prepare for the arrows, keeping Deva within his clenched fist. The giant's spine matched one of those prickly animals with quills along it's back. Safe under his arm, I saw more splinters enter his body. It would take more than a hundred arrows and the loss of a limb to overtake him.

With both hands, I grasped the solid handle of my grand new weapon. Amaziah's tool would be used against him. The weight felt good as I lifted the shaft to beat the jagged sphere into the body of the mighty angel. As I gashed more holes into the celestial being, light shot out from the exposed area. One swing followed another as I plowed through the flesh of the monster.

The final stroke made him burst in a blazing glow. He didn't vanish like the others, but sent out shock waves knocking down angels and jinn in its wake.

I tumbled back from the force of Amaziah's ruin. Once I found my balance, I rose and lifted my newly acquired weapon in the air, shouting victory.

"Followers of darkness, we will prevail!" I shouted. "Gather the equipment of the slaughtered angels and let's move forward to Earth."

"For Eve! For Earth! For us!" they chanted as we plowed through white robes to the blue and green planet.

As my troops advanced, I made note of my friends, checking for losses. The jinn around Abaddon kept their distance and appeared equally nervous as the angels. Zeus commanded a large army. I assumed he lost some, but I didn't know them well enough to count his losses.

The distinct sound of Sammael's crackling whip could not be heard. He was finally gone. I chuckled, pleased my accuser no longer surround me. Sammael started the process that led to my leaving heaven. Maybe I should thank him, but gratitude was far from describing my feelings toward Sammael.

I cared most for Deva and searched for his bronze wings and armor. I saw many crinkled wings on the warriors surrounded by scraps of material floating in space, but not Deva. Where could he be? The search for my friend made me pause in my advance toward Earth.

"Is everything all right?" Zeus asked.

"Yes, but I don't see Deva," I said.

"I do not believe he ever left the hand of the giant," Zeus said.

My eyes narrowed, and I felt regret in being so brutal in the use of my grand sphere through the massive flesh of the angel.

"Why didn't you free him?" I yelled at Zeus.

"He was not mine to protect," Zeus answered.

I growled. "How dare you imply I am incompetent!"

"I did no such thing. I didn't know who had been assigned to his care. If it is you, I stand by my original statement." Zeus took a moment; I assumed to consider his words. "My only apology is that you heard it."

The sound of a thousand trumpets cut off his words. I winced, annoying by the noise. What was happening? I needed to get to the front of my army to know what challenged us. There could be a whole army of heavenly giants. Or shields keeping them protected while they carefully sniped us from afar. The possibilities were endless.

When I arrived at the lead, my mouth fell open. Warriors riding horses floated behind the trumpet players Black studs with armored riders made the front fleet. Behind them, the stallion had red hair and carried riders with huge swords. In the next layer, the horses appeared pale and sickly.

Dumah's green fog protected them. For some reason, the smoke didn't turn them to stone the way the fog had in the practice room. Maybe they had already become statues and hovered above the atmosphere of Earth.

Phanuel rode one of the pale horses. I wanted him. The pain of his betrayal bubbled in my gut. He needed to be punished, but I didn't want him to be harmed. Being at the rear of the cavalry and on horseback would keep him safe.

Phanuel waited next to Jehovah who rode a white stallion. The beast's eyes were like flames of fire. Jehovah's white robes had been dipped in blood. The riders around Him called Him, "King of kings and Lord of lords."

Heavenly warriors chanted the same words over and over. Other white horses surrounded Jehovah. Their riders carried bows cocked with arrows and garland woven together to crown their heads.

"What do we do?" Zeus asked.

"Slaughter the animals and their riders. Then Earth will be ours!" I answered.

"For Eve! For Earth! For us!" we chanted.

As we charged toward the heavenly Calvary, they stampeded in our direction. To my surprise, when the hooves of the beasts trampled against my followers the force was strong enough to cause them to disappear rapidly. My number took a dramatic reduction within seconds.

"Fight these beasts the same as any other warrior," I instructed as the battle continued. "We will not let insignificant animals keep us from our goal."

They cheered at my words, but their eyes widened with fear. They needed proof the heavenly horses could be defeated.

I flew forward directly in line with a red-haired stallion. The soldier in the saddle raised his broadsword at my head. I wound the heavy bladed sphere dangling from the end of the handle. The dangerous ball slammed into the chest of the bronco.

To my surprise, my weapon continued through the beast without harming it. The same could not be said for the warrior on the animal's back. The spikes of the sphere slammed into the soldier, imploding him into nothing.

War quickly caged around me from every angle. Hopefully, my friends saw how to demolish their enemy.

I plowed my way through to the pale horses. The empty black eyes of Dumah stared back at me. I wanted to ignore the anxiety I felt creeping up my spine in response to his green fog coming at me from both sides. I lifted my weapon and swung it through Dumah's emerald gloom. The fog didn't move away.

How could I escape? Fleeing should never be an option. I needed to be courageous and not afraid. Narrowing my eyes, I charged directly at Dumah's pale horse.

"No!" Phanuel screamed.

Was he in trouble? Phanuel's voice echoed off the surrounding shields, making his location impossible to determine. Dumah's fog of death swirled closer. I looked to my left and right in search of Phanuel.

Directly in the middle of my back, my wings met. In that exact location, I felt the tip of a sharp blade puncture my flesh. Faster than I thought possible the spear of my enemy plunged through my body and poked out between my chest.

In the next breath, I vanished!

CHAPTER SIXTEEN

The heaven, even the heavens, are the LORD's:
but the earth hath he given to the children of men.
- Psalms 115: 16 (KJV)

I awoke to glaring light. I blinked rapidly, trying to remember what had happened. Looking at my chest, I saw where the bone-like armor cracked open. The protective barrier rested on my shoulders like a vest. A scar marred my front where I had been rammed through with a spear.

Could my assailant have been Phanuel? I refused to believe it. Maybe he felt the irrational need to protect Dumah from his impending doom. I would have destroyed the evil fog-yielding angel. Instead, Phanuel caused my own demise. He would pay!

Rage consumed me, which made the blinding glow in front of me irritating. I found myself in front of the golden gates of heaven. Guarded by Michael.

"God left you here?" I asked, but should have stated since the evidence provided the answer for me.

"I volunteered to be here," Michael said.

"Why? Didn't you want to take part in the battle?"

"Yes, but I knew many of your kind would be destroyed and arrive at the gate."

Once again, I was taken back by the humility displayed within the heavenly realm. Why would he give up what he wanted to take care of those defeated? The behavior seemed like something Jehovah would do.

"Shouldn't I have arrived at Elohim's feet? That's where Cassiel said he had been relocated."

"As one of His soldiers, then yes, that is where they are reinstated," Michael said. "For you and the fallen ones, you are outside the gate. There is no going back."

"The thought of returning has never crossed my mind," I said.

Michael nodded.

His gaze fell, and I wondered if my words had disappointed him.

Michael and Phanuel were my first allies but chosen against me. By default, that made them my enemies.

"You could join me," I offered. "I understand your loyalty, but it is misguided. It's only a matter of time before I take

Earth, the woman, and man. The world and everything in it will be mine. Come with me."

"It's not about things," Michael replied. "But what is right and wrong."

"Morality is what you make of it."

"You have made for yourself a pack of lies and called it true. Truth is not relative. It either is, or it is not." Michael crossed his arms over his chest, his sword in hand but not in a threatening manner.

"Best of luck, my friend," I said. "Be prepared to be shown otherwise."

"Godspeed," Michael said.

I soared away, confused by his closing words. He seemed to want to wish me well without saying so. My heart felt heavy, and I imagined Michael's felt the same. A time would come when Michael and I would fight, but today wasn't that day. Earth had to be the focus for now.

As I flew, the last of my tattered white robes fell from my body. I didn't need them anymore, but I missed my weapons. Later, I'd fashion new equipment, but there was something more important to do first.

I returned to the green and blue planet, with battles raging from every angle. Due to our ability to be reincarnated, the war could literally continue forever. I needed a different strategy to conquer Earth.

Before the start of the war, Sammael reported to me that God entered the Garden of Eden every morning to walk and fellowship with the man and woman. I followed the shadow of night and saw that daylight would reach the garden soon.

Being naked and unarmed, neither side knew which one I belonged to. I could use my knowledge of Jehovah's routine to build the trust of the heavenly guards who circled the hemisphere of Earth.

"Excuse me, gentlemen," I said.

"Halt!" shouted the middle guard with a curved staff thrust in front, blocking my entrance. He had layers of white robes trimmed in gold and thick bushy feathers on his wings.

I remembered him from the practice room. He removed his layers of robes for easier movement, and I tried to get him to use a different weapon, but he preferred his staff. His actions were swift and impressive. I wasn't sure how he'd destroy someone with the blunt tool, but he protected himself well.

My long blond locks had gone along with my beautiful reflective skin. I trusted they would not recognize me. The use of his name could build his trust.

"Uriel," I said. "Dawn is approaching, and I am to make way for Jehovah to commune with the humans."

The guard paused and glanced to the soldiers on his left and right. I could not blame him for not wanting to make the decision alone, but my window to make it to the man and woman before Jehovah narrowed quickly. Too much urgency would raise suspicion. I needed to be patient.

Uriel looked directly at me, and my breathing quickened. It took great care to wait as peacefully as possible.

"Where is your tunic?" asked the warrior next to Uriel.

"I thought it best not to wear white clothing with the war raging," I answered. "It would only put an unnecessary target on me. My mission is not to fight, but to prepare the way."

"Very well. Complete your mission," said the other angel.

Uriel nodded and moved his staff to allow me to enter.

"I will." I cast down my face to hide my smirk.

Passing through the Earth's atmosphere, I immediately smelled the moisture in the air and the saltiness of the ocean. I loved this planet and wanted it as much as I coveted the woman. Once in the garden, she'd be the one I approach.

The couple walked through the nursery hand in hand. I wondered if either heard the battle raging above the night sky. While fluttering through the sweet flowers, I thought about what I'd say to Eve. I wanted the man to be with her to gather them both at the same time.

I whispered in the wind gaining the woman's attention. Her eyes drew to a serpent twisting through the branches of the forbidden tree. The creature was craftier than the other wild animals. Orange and blue scales ran down its long spine creating a diamond pattern against his skin. Raised plates along the reptile's neck met on his back where wings flapped, helping him to stand erect.

"Woman," I whispered.

She leaned nearer to the creature as I entered through the snake's tail. The bends and curves of the animal suited me well and provided another form to cover my nakedness. Maybe the humans would not care since they were also unclothed.

Being inside the varmint helped me blend in with the natural surroundings. I moved the legs of the serpent to climb through the branches closer to the woman.

Eve had taken a liking to a white lamb. The animal skipped about at her feet and curled into her side when she wanted rest. She often spoke to the gentle beast and the wooly creature communicated back to the woman in a hushed whisper. The remarkable human understood the animal.

"Do you need something?" the woman asked the serpent.

I needed her to see the uselessness of God. I needed her to trust me. I needed her and the man to show how easily God's plans could be destroyed. Then I would be proven as greater. The remaining angels would flock to Zophos. Jehovah would have no choice but to hang in shame.

By giving the humans clear instructions, it made it easy for me to create doubt. Once I knew I had more abilities than God, His supposed greatness paled in comparison to my own. It became the catalyst that brought my followers to me.

Elohim didn't allow us to simply leave, but scooped the lava and poured it over us. His actions destroyed my beauty! I vowed revenge and would permanently scar His beloved humans. I needed something greater than she could possibly imagine.

I hissed as I spoke, "Did God really say, 'You must not eat from any tree in the garden'?" The hand of the serpent circled the stem of a ripe fruit from within the forbidden tree.

The woman answered, "We may eat fruit from the trees in the garden, but God did say 'You must not eat fruit from the tree in the middle of the garden, and you must not touch it, or you will die.'"

Maybe the man had told her in error, or she added the rule herself to keep the temptation further from her grasp. Regardless of how she came to believe the error, I saw the certainty in her eyes. She believed every word to be absolute truth.

"You certainly will not die," I said.

I liked that they had the ability to make choices. The skill gave them the option to make mistakes. Same for Phanuel making it possible he might have relayed God's instruction incorrectly to me.

For a moment, I thought of my lost servant. Being angry at him took too much effort, and I refused to believe he had intentionally contributed to my peril. I missed him. When God's plan crumbled, Phanuel would gain the courage to join me.

I continued. "For God knows when you eat from this tree your eyes will be opened, and you will be like God, knowing good and evil."

I wanted to show her the beauty that true wisdom could bring her. Knowledge would exceed her charm and elegance.

She brushed her long black hair from her shoulder. The locks snuggled against her tan naked back, leaving her chest exposed.

Desire bubbled up within me. Through determination and patience, I brought the lust down to a simmer not wanting the feeling to boil over and destroy my plan. The quick tongue of the serpent darted out to taste the fruit. I felt hunger within the creature and a longing to consume the sweet flavor.

Her eyes lingered over the produce within the tree. She calculated its allure and ripeness. The fruit had a rich smell which meant it would most likely be pleasing to the tongue. Her hand quivered as she reached toward the tree. She brought her hand back to her chest and then out once more. The tip of her finger traced the bark on its trunk.

She looked over her shoulder at her mate who stood with her but said nothing. Adam rested against the trunk of the Tree of Knowledge of Good and Evil, watching the Tree of Life and it's magic. The rotation of the leaves colors from green, yellow and red, to brown and spurts of purple blossoms could mesmerize someone for hours and make them lose sight of anything else around them.

The serpent remained focused. He knew the instructions the Lord God gave to Adam, but didn't think to make the woman pause. Had the creature tried I would have stopped him from speaking. No attempt to correct Eve came from anyone or anything.

What more should I say? Too much encouragement could strike a chord of guilt and cause her to stop. I felt the closeness of the celestial realm. The war above halted as both sides watched me with earnest.

With a trembling hand her fingers wrapped around the fruit and broke it from the tree. Her body trembled and her breath left in a gasp as her other hand fell upon her breast. The man's gaze left the mesmerizing Tree of Life to follow her hand and became transfixed by her beauty.

Eve said moments before she could not touch it or it would result in her immediate death. As she stared at the fruit in her palm her eyebrows slowly crinkled toward each other and her lips curled into a frown. Her shoulders slumped forwards.

I watched her faith in God crumble. For whatever reason, she fully believed she should have died.

The fruit wobbled within her shaking hand. For a moment I thought the produce would escape and roll into the green grass. No! She needed to eat it.

Adam might have relayed God's message to her clumsily, but I knew Phanuel had been accurate in his delivery to me. Once she ate, her eyes would be fully opened. I didn't understand why God kept knowledge from His creation, but it made me want to give it even more.

I continued to feel the gaze of the angels guarding Earth. The man and woman were God's chosen ones. He made them in Their image and therefore should be indestructible. Once again, the heavenly realm had it wrong. No one, heavenly or human, was beyond my grasp.

Humans would be enlightened in the same way I had delivered my followers from heaven. They'd see my superiority in every way.

Colorful leaves from the Tree of Life left their branches and floated toward the trio of angels who allowed me to enter Earth.

Uriel clutched his long staff, ready to fight. "Lucifer! Come from the serpent and leave the presence of Earth," he demanded.

The creature reared onto his hind legs. Its tiny wings kept him stable within the branches of the tree. I felt the curiosity of the animal, wanting to know Eve's decision.

"Isn't it better to know the fate of God's elite?" I asked.

"Not from you," the other angel said. "For you are a liar and a thief."

"I only take what is already mine as you will soon see."

The third angel glared and readied his long bow with an arrow. If he shot me I could return, but what of the serpent?

The creature backed against the security of the trunk. Though the angels were ready and able, they'd wait for God's command before influencing the humans.

If God was truly all-knowing, He knew the actions of Eve and me. He could have arrived in time to stop us. Or he had the power to simply speak His command. He never said a word.

All watched as the courageous woman took the fruit to her red lips and bit down. She licked the sweet nectar and offered the same to her mate, who stood silently with her.

"Adam, eat." She held out the produce to him. Her pulse raced beneath her flesh. She remained strong and vibrant, despite God's promise of death.

He saw the bite taken from the fruit. His voice remained lodged in his throat as his eyes widened and he reached for her with his other hand.

Anger radiated from his body. With defiance, he took the fruit and ate as well.

A collective gasp rang from every corner of Heaven and Earth.

I had defeated God.

"I am the champion!"

CHAPTER SEVENTEEN

"Be sober, be vigilant; because your adversary the devil, as a roaring lion, walketh about, seeking whom he may devour."
- 1 Peter 5:8 (KJV)

Now, nothing stopped me. From this day forward, I became the ruler and prince of Earth! The man and woman had eaten from the fruit the Lord told them not to. I felt my multitudes strengthen as a flood of angels joined my ranks. Surly, Phanuel would be among them.

The woman held one hand to her chest, and then the other arm joined in covering herself.

What was she doing? Nothing in Heaven or Earth was as radiant as her. Why would she suddenly feel the need to mask her body?

"Eve, you're naked," whispered the man.

He must be dumb because they had always been naked.

"So are you," she replied.

Clearly, these two were not the brightest in the patch. Together, they scrambled together a pile of loose vegetation. Their hands trembled causing them to drop several leaves before mending them together to make coverings for themselves.

I didn't know everything about foliage, but the Tree of Life had taught me leaves went through cycles. They started off strong and green, but would quickly wither and become brittle and break. The petals would not make for durable clothing.

As daylight broke, the ground shook. Trumpets sounded, drawing mine and the human's attention to the sky. A cloud came through the layers of the trees who bowed before their Maker. The garden filled with smoke and the rocks cries out in praises to God. The Lord had arrived.

He had been arrogant and foolish to trust the weak humans to obey. His scarred feet walked through the soft grass as his white robes trailed behind him. A breeze followed him, sweeping away the smoke. Around Jehovah, the birds sang. The chorus grew louder as he approached.

I remained within the serpent, watching and waiting. The man and woman also huddled together within a strong tree. Their self-made garments allowed them to blend in with their environment but didn't cover their smell. The fruit's sweet nectar remained on their face and hands like a sweet perfume.

The Lord God called to the man, "Where art thou?"

Though in human form, the Spirit remained in the morning fog and Elohim spoke for him, giving Him a deeper voice. I felt the respect the sound deserved.

So much for an all-knowing God. Why ask such an absurd question? Yes, they camouflaged themselves within the tree but were easy to find.

The man climbed down from the tree. He approached God with his hands clenched into fists and his muscles flexed with tension making him appear ready for battle except, his shoulders slumped forward. He gazed at the ground.

Adam answered, "I heard you in the garden, and I was afraid because I was naked; so I hid."

"Who told you that thou were naked?" God asked. "Have thou eaten from the tree of which I commanded thee not to eat?"

The man said, "The woman You put here with me. She gave me some fruit from the tree, and I ate it."

I chuckled to myself. Even the ignorant man knew God had made a mistake in trusting them and placed the blame where it belonged.

The woman glared at Adam.

His face would not meet hers.

Then the Lord God said to the woman, "What is this thou have done?"

With her head bowed, her long hair cloaked over her shoulders and down her back. She ran her fingers through the strands like the motion made her feel safe and secure.

The woman said, "The serpent deceived me, and I ate."

Yes, I did!

I'd gladly tell anyone who asked of my accomplishments. I started the day thinking I'd be victorious in the skies but instead came directly to the main source walking on Earth.

So the Lord God turned his head to me. I assumed he heard my boastful thoughts and hissed in approval. Let Him continue to be forever mocked and shamed!

The Lord God said to the serpent, "Because thou have done this, thy art cursed more than cattle, and more than every beast of the field. On thy belly thy shall go, and thou shall eat dust all the days of thy life."

Jehovah walked to the water and scooped mud from the bottom. I stiffened remembering the hot lava Elohim poured over me shattering my radiance. God returned to the tree. Capturing the serpent by the tail, He ran his hand along the twisting body of the snake smearing the mud across its flesh. The animal's legs and wings broke from his torso leaving only its withering frame.

The serpent hissed. I felt the creature's anger and regret at not warning the woman. Who knew God would hold the animal accountable for his inaction?

Did God know the creature didn't have a say in the role it played? It's not like I asked its permission before entering its body. Once again, God was making a fool of himself and should be scorned. I started to leave the reptile to let him speak for himself, but the Lord continued.

"And I shall put enmity between thee and the woman and between thy seed and hers. He shall bruise thy head, and thou shall bruise His heel."

What did He mean by such an announcement? God spoke to the future like He knew what would happen. He didn't know where the man and woman had been hiding only moments before and didn't have the ability to peer into the future and know what would happen. For a moment, I thought of Jehovah's scars and how He said they were yet to come. It made no sense.

Regardless of the lack of logic, the man and woman nodded and smiled at one another. God's message gave them peace and hope for tomorrow.

"Tell me what to do," Adam said to God.

God took the man by the hand and showed him how to bring an offering to Him and to cover their sin. They gathered stones and lumped them one after another until the collection reached the man's waist. The Lord called the pilean alter.

The humans could not be redeemed on their own. They had made their choice to reject God. I'd teach them to serve me, or they'd pursue one of my other followers, but their interaction with God would never be the same. The relationship could not be fixed.

The Lord said, "Starting with a burnt-offering, thou shall offer a male without blemish. Lay thy hand on the head of the burnt-offering, and it shall be acceptable as atonement for thee."

The man called a young bull to him and found the animal to be without spot. God sharpened a stone and brought the tool to Adam. The small bull laid within the arms of the man in perfect peace for there was no reason for the creature to have fear. The human followed God's instruction and brought the blade across the neck of the bull, but not deep enough to kill the animal. The bull billowed in pain. Blood spilled onto Adam's skin.

Eve screamed and covered her face.

"My child, thy must look and remember," God said. He took her hand and brought her to the wounded animal, trying to flee Adam's grasp. With Eve's fingers, God snapped the neck of the bull. Drops of blood sprayed the man and woman. God used the rest of the dark liquid to bathe the altar in red.

"The animal's blood is shed for thee," the Lord God said. Blood flowed from the dead animal along each stone until the liquid pooled on the ground. The slaughter of the helpless animal was brutal.

Tears dripped down the face of Adam and Eve.

Wild cats approached and sniffed the air. A lion licked his lips and leaned back on its haunches. Death had entered the world, and it appeared many creatures within the animal kingdom liked the concept.

God stripped the skin from the bull and took it to the river to be cleansed. For a moment the crystal-clear stream flowed red. The fat and organs of the helpless animal were separated and added to the altar. The Lord God stretched out his hand and caused fire to shoot from His fingertips to burn the sacrifice. Juices bubbled and grease popped from the flames.

"Thou shall make atonement for sin, and then be forgiven," the Lord God said.

Adam added sticks to the flame until it consumed the whole bull. Smoke billowed and the odor of burnt fat and organs filled the air.

I thought the sulfur of hell was bad. It was paradise compared to this repulsive stench. I grew tired of hearing the woman cry and heave as she vomited from the gore. I left the confines of the snake, but stayed close. Curiosity kept me from leaving. God could not work his way out of this predicament, but I wanted to watch Him try.

Throughout the garden, the man and woman gathered grain as the Lord asked them to do. With sturdy stones, they ground the corn into flour. God showed them how to press the seeds to create oil. Sweat pooled on the man's forehead and ran down his face and arms.

They mixed the flour and oil together and added a portion to the burning animal. They placed the remaining portion on a flat rock and added it to the altar to cook. A pleasant aroma lifted from the bread as it baked.

Finally, something good happened. I didn't trust God for a second, but based on my standards it appeared He was losing His mind. Once the dough fully cooked, God removed the bread from the fire and broke the loaf into two pieces. He handed one to Adam and the other Eve.

"Eat, and listen," the Lord said.

The woman wiped tears from her eyes. She tore a piece of the bread and ate it. The white lamb by her side nibbled the crumbs landing on the woman's lap.

"Eve, bring me the animal near thee."

The woman gathered the lanky lamb into her arms and approached the Lord. He reached for the blade that had sliced through the neck of the goat.

She took a step back. "Are you going to hurt him?" she asked.

"Yes, Eve. It must be done."

Why? Blood being shed solved nothing.

Her eyes welled up with tears, and she buried her face into the wool of the animal.

"Can we take its fur and spare his life?" Adam asked.

"For the payment of sin, blood must be shed. Thou must assemble and offer a lamb or bull of the herd for a sin-offering. Thou must lay thy hands on the head of the animal as it is slaughtered."

God had become cruel. No, he always had been. He took from the woman an animal she loved, not because he needed too, but because He could.

"Please, my Lord. There must be another way," the woman begged.

"There will be." God stretched out his hand and caught her tear in his scarred palm. "I promise thee; there will be. Today, I will show compassion to the lamb. Remember the sacrifice the animal almost made. I will accept two pigeons, one for a sin-offering and the other for a burnt-offering. The burnt-offering has already been completed so only one bird is now needed."

With his powerful hands, God showed Adam how to wring the bird's neck without severing it. He sprinkled drops of blood on the side of the altar, while the rest of the blood he drained out at the base of the altar.

While the smell of burnt animals filled the sky, God prepared the dried skin of the bull to make clothing for his creation. The man wore loins around his waist. For the woman, she had the same plus additional garments covering her breasts.

It saddened me for her beauty to be concealed. What did knowing good and evil have to do with modesty? It made no sense to me.

As the heavenly realm saw God's plan crumble, I felt my flock increase. I wanted to know who had joined me.

CHAPTER EIGHTEEN

*"Put on the whole armor of God,
that ye may be able to stand against the wiles of the devil."*
- Ephesians 6:11 (KJV)

Fluttering by the fires of hell, their light made the halls appear blue, purple, or orange depending on the heat of the flames. I enjoyed the warmth of the lava which surrounded my dark palace.

From what I could tell those who came with me the first time remained, plus several more legions came after the fall of man. In total, one-third of what had once been the heavenly realm were now within my halls.

The new members worked well with one another and enjoyed the alliance they formed. I was proud of my followers. They created new songs and sang them in my honor and to each other.

As long as the music wasn't to God, I didn't care who they directed their praise toward. If their adoration was to themselves, they could only do that because of me, and therefore it sounded pleasing.

The only one who appeared to not be at ease was Deva.

"Is everything all right?"

Deva narrowed his eyes and paused for a moment. "I have not adjusted to my new name and purpose."

"Give it time; ease will come. Have you thought of how you will spread your good news?"

"Some."

"Once the population on Earth grows you'll have billions to influence."

"Thank you for this task," Deva said. "Is there anything specific you wish for me to share?"

"That is up to you, my friend. Make it your own." I smiled at him and placed my hand on his shoulder to be a comforting gesture.

"Very well, then." He bowed and backed away.

I felt the heaviness of his thoughts but not the details. Deva needed more. I needed Phanuel. Surely he had joined me after witnessing God's creation be influenced by my charms. He'd be the apprentice that would give Deva his purpose.

"I must find Phanuel," I said out loud to myself.

My light had grown dim but was enough to help me see every corner of the darkened palace. Sulfur and smoke billowed below, and several moved throughout the ashes. Through the gray stone archway, I left the castle and fluttered to them.

Maalik's long black hair drug across the hardened rocks and sizzled when the strands fell over in the hot molten. Others nearby helped to lengthen the dwelling place. He knew more would come the same as I did. I appreciated his service, but wondered about his allegiances.

"Who do you serve?" I asked.

"The darkness," answered Maalik.

I only saw his chin, the rest of his face covered by long bangs.

"And what of my light? Does it bother you?"

"It makes no difference to me," he answered.

"What of God?" I asked.

"I have no need for him. Whether it be you or god, it is equal. One not greater or lesser than the other."

"Fair enough. As you were."

"Phanuel is not here," Maalik said.

"How do you know?"

"My men and I have watched everyone enter."

"How did you know I was looking for him?" I asked, tired of angels being able to pry into my thoughts without them being wanted.

"I heard you through the open window." He gestured to the gray stone archway I flew through to approach him. "You have assembled quite a following; you should be proud."

Smoke billowed in his face which he shooed away with his pointed staff.

"I am," I said.

"And yet, you want another."

"There will be more to come. For that, I have no doubt."

"You and I agree."

I didn't like that Maalik seemed to know more than me, making his humility difficult to understand. He never gloated but stated things matter-of-factly. I appreciated his honesty. In a world where absolutes blurred, I liked knowing I had someone I could trust.

"I know where he is," Maalik said.

I stepped closer in anticipation. "Tell."

"After the man and woman tasted the fruit to know good and evil, the lord god didn't want to risk them eating from the tree of life and living forever. He—"

"Wait! How do you know this?"

"God said it. I listen to everything around me."

"Continue."

"The man and woman were banished from the Garden of Eden and he commanded Adam to work the ground and to feed himself by his own strength."

"The anger of God can not be holy when He does these things to His creation." I shook my head and clenched my fist. "I'd never treat them so poorly no matter what they did."

"To keep them from returning, god placed a cherub to guard the entrance. That angel is Phanuel."

"How could he do such a thing!" My voice became swallowed by the bubbling lava.

"Do you mean god or Phanuel?" Maalik asked.

"Both," I answered. "How do you know this?"

"As I said, I watch. I am neither of god nor of you. I have no allegiance and therefore keep an open mind to all possibilities."

"Regardless of whose side you think you're on, trust me. It's my side." I gave him a grin, which he didn't return. "Thanks for the information."

He nodded slightly.

I left hell and found myself missing its heat. It warmed me and made me feel at home. I had a final stop to make, and then I'd return.

As I approached the blue and green planet, I noticed the guards no longer surrounded it like last time. Maybe, God had finally accepted my earthly reign, giving up on His creation. The Earth was mine, and all that remained in it. That included Phanuel.

Most of the animals left the garden with the man and woman to be cared for by them. They needed protection from the wilder beasts who enjoyed the smell of blood in the air and grew to like the taste of meat and bones.

On the east side of the Garden of Eden Phanuel stood guard. The waves of his long wings rustled his blond hair. He wore no shirt, and his strong muscles might have been intimidating to someone who didn't know about Phanuel's gentle spirit. Next to the angel stood a broadsword with fire leaping from its tip. It remained poised on its own between the Tree of Life and Phanuel.

"So, is this God's version of finally giving you a weapon?" I asked. "In case you can not guard the tree on your own, you have flaming assistance. Clever."

"Lucifer, what do you want?" Phanuel asked.

The Tree of Life behind him continued its never-ending cycle. The strong green leaves turned to red and yellow before crumbling to the ground in a pile of brown. I hated to admit the sight mesmerized me. I could stare at the tree for ages.

"Luc?" Phanuel brought my attention back to him.

"Did you have me destroyed in battle?" The question wasn't what I had come to say, but I needed an answer. Doubt had been gnawing on my nerves for what felt like days.

"No, I tried to save you." His eyes fell to my chest where the scar remained between my breasts.

"Then who administered the blow?"

"Gabriel," answered Phanuel, "with Barachiel's spear."

I didn't expect such brutality from the gentle angel. I must have struck a nerve for him to be so hostile.

Phanuel swallowed, revealing his nervousness.

He should be uneasy. It gave me strength. His respect for me remained strong, but I could not feel his emotions the way I used to when we were on the same side.

I missed him. The emotion made me weak, and I didn't like the feeling but realized it might be used to my advantage. The more truth I shared with him, the more he'd put his faith fully in me.

"I wish you were with me. Phanuel, we belong together."

"Yes, we do," Phanuel admitted.

"Then you will come!" Convincing him proved to be much easier than I initially thought. He simply needed someone to encourage and lead him.

"I can not." His beautiful face fell toward the ground. The sparking sword cast light across his features.

I placed my hand on his shoulder. "You can do anything."

"Including stay?"

"Yes, if that's what you want," I said. Phanuel's shoulders shook and his eyes filled with agony. "Sometimes, doing the right thing hurts. Be free, Phanuel."

"Yes, of course." He took a long and deep breath. "I warred within on whether to tell you, but there is something you must know."

I nodded, staying quiet to not interrupt his words.

"Jehovah told me about his scars and how he received them."

"What?" I asked, wishing I had kept my own advice and been quiet, but I could not move past the shock of his words.

"They are for mankind. He will save them."

"No, he didn't. I watched animals be brutally murdered to pay for Adam's sin."

"Yes, the animals will be used to foreshadow a greater provider. God will explain in further detail, one of the goats will be the sacrificed as a sin offering for his people, and another goat will be released unharmed into the wilderness. The sin offering will provide forgiveness, while the other goat granted the removal of sin."

"That is ridiculous! Jehovah didn't sacrifice anything. I can't believe he has you so deceived. He has lied to you, Phanuel."

"You do not understand."

"Enlighten me." I crossed my arms over my chest and waited to be impressed feeling confident nothing Phanuel said would surprise me.

Phanuel circled the standing sword. "You do not want to hear my words."

"You look like a spoiled animal Eve used to coddle." I sneered, unsure why I ever paid him so much attention. "I don't care about the lies God has told you."

"They are not lies; it's the truth. Lucifer, you didn't win. You've been following God's plan. You were created for this purpose." He stepped in front of the blazing sword, his back straight. "Do you think it surprised Them when you turned away? Do you think They didn't know from the moment you were created?"

He paused, and I knew I was supposed to speak, but I didn't know what to say. The silence hung between us until I finally found my voice.

"You are under the assumption God knows all," I said. "I don't believe that's true."

"That's the thing about truth. It does not require belief to be true. It is true because it is so, regardless of what anyone else thinks." Phanuel smiled displaying the same confidence he had since circling the strange flaming sword.

Michael had said something similar.

"Well, isn't that convenient?"

"Listen, Lucifer. God will establish an elaborate system to cover the sins of His people."

"They are not His! They are MINE!" My voice echoed from every direction.

"Some, yes, but not all. God will set up a covenant with His people. They will be His and different from everyone else. God will make them be so by giving them commandments to follow that will set them apart. The animals died in place of the sinner, but later Jehovah will come and leave Heaven to dwell among men. He will die as the final lamb. He will be the ultimate sacrificial substitute once for all time."

It was absolute craziness. I remembered asking Jehovah about his scars, and he said he received them voluntarily. One day I'd know how he was able to be pierced.

As much as I didn't like what Phanuel had told me, I believed it to be true. I must raise up my army and prepare for the day when God made the ultimate sacrifice.

I'll be ready.

THE END

Please take time to review and continue for a sneak preview of the next release from JJ Liniger.

Find out more about JJ at journeywithjewels.wordpress.com and www.facebook.com/JJLiniger/.

For free stories, a sneak peek at new novels, and more, join the email list at JJLiniger.com and journeywithjewels@gmail.com

Enjoy a special preview of JJ's next novel, *God's Will.*

Dear Reader

Theologians have debated many of the themes throughout this book for centuries:

Why did God create Satan at all?

How did a heavenly, all-good angel get the idea to sin?

Once Satan had the idea, what made him think it was a good idea?

Once sin entered the world, why go through the sacrifices? Why not skip directly to Jesus?

Why give us the ability to sin at all?

I can't answer all of these questions, but I am willing to take a stab at some of them.

Scripture leaves little doubt in the omniscience of God, Job 37:16, Psalms 139:2-4 & 147:5, Proverbs 5:21, Isaiah 46:9-10 and 1 John3:19-20. He knows everything that will happen as well as everything that happened in the past. Therefore, it is clear God knew Satan would fall the moment He created him.

So, then why create Lucifer at all?

That question is not so clearly answered. However, we know God does not (and can not) make mistakes otherwise He wouldn't be perfect. So, for whatever reason, the fall of Satan was part of God's sovereign plan from the beginning.

Colossians 1:16 tells us that "for by Him all things were created that are in Heaven and that are on Earth, visible and invisible. All things were created through Him and for Him." As crazy as it seems, no other answer fits the characteristics of God than it to be God's plan for Satan to exist.

God didn't cause Satan to rebel but gave him free will to do so. I'm not sure about you, but I like having the ability to praise God or reject God. And I think God likes that we choose Him for Him, not because there isn't any other option. We know in all things God works for the good of those who love him. "All things" includes the horrible things we often contribute to Satan.

At the end of day one, God declared all He created to be "good" and that included Lucifer. If that isn't clear enough, at the end of the week, he declares all His creation "very good." Lucifer's rebellion does not change God's original intent from good to evil. God uses Satan's evilness to bring Him glory and fulfill His purpose (1 Timothy 1:20, 1 Corinthians 5:5).

There are other examples in scripture where God permits evil to bring a greater blessing. In Genesis 50:20, Joseph attributes the evil actions of his brothers (they sold him into slavery) as part of God's plan to bring him to Egypt and save his family. God allows Satan to torture Job, for him to be an example to those who read the story and gain wisdom. Jesus' crucifixion was brutal, and it is clear Satan was involved in Jesus' execution (entering Judas to betray Jesus and festering the crowds to choose death for Jesus), but through Jesus' death and resurrection God has provided for us the ultimate victory.

God's plan for salvation didn't start with the fall of man. I have a hard time imagining God going, "Adam, no! Now what?" because He didn't do that. According to Revelation 13:8, our names were written in the Book of Life before the creation of the world. God knew because it is His plan.

Why did God choose this for His plan? I don't know. It seems so messed up, right? And with that thought, we need to be extremely careful. The moment we believe things would have been better if God had done this or that, or **not** done this or that, we have aligned our thoughts exactly with Satan. Lucifer believes he knows more than God and would be better than God. I know it looks obvious that things would be better if Satan had never existed, but I'm going to trust God enough to say it is better for Satan to be amongst us, or the devil wouldn't be here.

God's plan started with sacrifices and the clothing of Adam and Eve with fur. Then through the Old Testament, we have the sacrificial system. The Burnt Offering illustrated complete surrender to God's will (Leviticus 1:9). Jesus did the same when he told the father "not my will, but yours". The Grain Offering represented obedience of sinless service (without leaven) and communion with God. That is why Jesus calls him the "bread of life" and "salt of the earth" because he *is* the sinless offering. The Peace Offering symbolizes intimate friendship and reconciliation. Jesus demonstrated that relationship with the father and then provided a way for us to have the same through his death on the cross. The details listed in the Sin Offering are the most obvious that point to Jesus. The author of Hebrews points to this sacrificial system and acknowledges the correlation. The final sacrifice is the Guilt Offering, which is to heal the damage done by sin.

Through the sacrifices, during the Old Testament, we have a strange correlation and foreshadowing of Jesus, described as "the lamb of God". If you've never looked into the Jewish yearly feasts, it's something worth doing. The foreshadowing in the Passover, Unleavened Bread, Pentecost, Day of Atonement, and others are truly fascinating. You'll be able to see God's plan unfold in a way you've never noticed before.

Sometimes we need to be okay in not knowing. There are things we will never fully understand until we are face to face with God. But, I trust God's plan is wonderful, and it stretches into eternity. There are things for us to ponder and then come to realize, we don't know. Thank God, He is in control!

I do not claim to know the answers and this book is certainly fiction, but I have tried to stay as scripturally accurate as I can. Through diving into the mind of Satan, I feel like I have gained a grasp of him and on God.

You might ask, why would I want to dive into the mind of Satan? The answer is both complicated and simple. The main reason is because I believe he has a fascinating story to tell. As believers, it is important we understand our adversary to defend ourselves properly. We need to understand our opponent to know best how to defeat him. Ignoring him doesn't solve anything. Enter this journey with an open mind. I pray the end results will bring you closer to God.

Satan is a fascinating character. I have attempted to thoroughly demonstrate his many attributes. Most people focus on his evilness, which should never be ignored, it's important to remember he started off good. He had and still has the ability to make choices, to strategize and plan, and to communicate clearly but not necessarily truthfully (Matthew 4:1-11).

Satan is a real being; I hesitate to call him a person because he is not human. Our struggle is not against flesh and blood, but against the rulers, against the powers, against the world forces of this darkness, against the spiritual forces of wickedness in the heavenly places.

How can there be wickedness in heavenly places? This verses directly before this one tells us to put on the armor of God so we can withstand the schemes of the devil. Satan is the wickedness that originated in heaven. While in the presence of God I believe something dramatic happened to Lucifer which made him believe God to be evil. For God to be wrong and by default Satan be right.

I believe his twisted way of thinking started with a desire to do good, to make himself and those around him better. In Lucifer's mind, God held him back and kept him from his true potential. Once he defied God, then he became a missionary of darkness with a new "truth" and insight that would make life better for all. His actions are misguided and wrong, but originates from good intentions. He was able to lure one-third of the angels with his version of "goodness" and he wants to conquer the entire world.

One of my greatest fears is I have presented Lucifer's argument so well you begin to believe what he says to be true. Therefore, a reminder of his true nature is important.

Satan is our accuser. According to Revelation 12:10 he takes pleasure in accusing God's children of sin day and night. The beginning of Job is another example of him entering the throne room of God for the sole purpose of making accusations not against God but us as well. He knows our salvation can never be lost, but finds joy in filling the believer with doubts. The saint's allegiance to God is a personal insult to Satan, and he takes delight in tormenting God's children.

Satan is incredibly smart and disguises himself in light, which makes him a deceiver. For some, he blinds them completely from the work of Jesus. For others, he changes the gospel (2 Corinthians 4:4) so that people believe to be following Jesus when they are not. The many variations of Christianity is the work of Satan. If he can distract us and have us bicker about specific nuances throughout scripture, then our focus is no longer on Jesus. I believe Satan considers that a win for him.

Satan is patient. He waits, like a lion crouched in the grass, so its helpless prey will not see him coming until it is too late. This also makes Satan our oppressor. His actions are calculated. His goal is to turn people's focus away from God. Not only because he hates God, but because Satan fully believes God is the one who leads others astray. The best way to do that is to distort God's truth.

Satan is a tempter and tries to do the same to Jesus. Imagine the level of arrogance it would take to look Jesus in the face and say, "I'm better. Pick me." That is basically what Satan does. If he thinks he has a chance at tempting Jesus, then he believes even more so that we can and will fall astray. Sometimes a sinful Christian can do more for Satan than anyone else.

Though Satan is intelligent, he is not creative and can be seen throughout scripture as imitating God. In 2 Corinthians 11:13-15, it's another example of him disguising himself as God. He will not show his true nature because his deception would be obvious. He might consider himself a "messenger of truth," but he hides behind the real Truth as he counterfeits it with lies.

Which leads to his next attribute, he is a liar and the father of lies (John 8:44). His words can not be trusted. He will use the same technique on you and me as he did on Eve. He loves to make us believe something about God's character that is not true and then when God doesn't perform as we think He should, then our faith in Him has been crushed. I know when this happens to me, if I am honest I will see that God didn't fail, but I put conditions on Him that shouldn't have been there.

Seeing that Satan is very much real and he is certainly not good. What are we do to? How do we protect ourselves? The Bible tells us exactly what to do. We are to put on the full armor of God. We have the Belt of Truth, the Breastplate of Righteousness, Boots of Peace, the Shield of Faith, the Helmet of Salvation, and the Sword, which is the Word of God. We are to pray and to communicate with God.

God has given us everything we need. But most importantly, he has given us Jesus. Romans 3:23 tells us for all have sinned and fallen short of the glory of God. No one is perfect. Is sin really that big of a deal? Yes, it is. Romans 6:23 tells us for the wages of sin is death, but the gift of God is eternal life in Christ Jesus our Lord. God provided a solution to the sin problem because being a good person is not good enough.

Ephesians 2:8,9 says "For by grace you have been saved by faith. And that, not of yourselves. It is the gift of God, not of works. Lest any man should boast." Jesus is the answer, the only answer. We are saved by confessing our sins and repent.

The first step toward repentance is to be sorry for the wrong things we've done.

Romans 5:8 tells us God demonstrates His own love toward us, in that while we were still sinners, Christ died for us. God took care of us. The solution is simple! Romans 10:9 says if you confess with your mouth the Lord Jesus and believe in your heart God has raised Him from the dead, you will be saved. Place your faith in God's son, Jesus Christ who died and paid for our sins on the cross.

If you would like to do that, I encourage you to pray something like this:

Dear God, I come to you in the name of Jesus. I acknowledge that I am a sinner in need of a savior. I am sorry for my sins, and I need your forgiveness. I believe that your son Jesus Christ shed his blood on the cross and died for my sins. I am now willing to turn from my sin and want Jesus to guide me. This moment, I accept Jesus Christ as my own personal Savior. Amen.

According to God's Word, right now you are saved, though it has nothing to do with the prayer, but it is by faith. Take a moment and thank God for his unlimited grace. You are now fully equipped to withstand the schemes of the devil. Remember, Satan is powerful and evil. Dive into the scriptures and form your battle plan.

Stand confident that you have the King of kings and the Lord of lords on your side. One day Satan will be cast forever into the lake of fire!

God is and will be victorious!!

Please take time to review and continue for a sneak preview of the next release from JJ Liniger.

Discussion Guide

Its okay to not know the answers, theologians have debated many of the themes throughout this book for centuries: Grab a group of friends. Once together, challenge and learn from one another. As the body of Christ we can build each other up.

1. Since God knew Lucifer would rebel and take other angels with him, why did God create Satan at all?

2. What do you think Satan was like before his fall?

3. How did a heavenly, all-good angel get the idea to sin?

4. What was Lucifer's root problem or sin?

5. Once Satan had the idea, what made him think it was a good idea?

6. Why did God allow the angels to rebel?

7. What did Michael and Gabriel see in God that Lucifer missed?

8. Do you think the "good" angels tried to convert Lucifer and his flock back to God? Could the fallen angels return to God?

9. Colossians 1:16 tells us that "for by Him all things were created that are in Heaven and that are on Earth, visible and invisible. All things were created through Him and for Him." Do you believe this includes Satan?

10. Why did God allow Adam and Eve to listen to Satan?

11. What was the real purpose of the "Tree of Knowledge of Good and Evil"?

12. What was the purpose of the "Tree of Life"? What happened to it?

13. Why did God add those two restricted trees to the garden?

14. What were the progressive steps that resulted in Eve's sin? What can we learn from her example?

15. Are Adam and Eve in Heaven or Hell? Why?

16. Satan loves to make us believe something about God's character that is not true and then when God doesn't perform as we think He should, then our faith in Him has been crushed. Can you give an example of how this happened in your life?

17. Once sin entered the world, why go through the sacrifices? Why did God choose this for His plan? Why not skip directly to Jesus?

18. Why give us the ability to sin at all?

19. Are people destined to go to hell?

20. According to Ephesians, our struggle is not against flesh and blood, but against the rulers, against the powers, against the world forces of this darkness, against the spiritual forces of wickedness in the heavenly places. How can there be wickedness in heavenly places?

21. Can Satan read our minds?

22. How does Satan deal with everyone in the world at the same time?

23. What character qualities of Lucifer surprised you the most?

24. How is Satan your accuser?

25. How does Lucifer now react to the pain and suffering happening in hell?

26. Does Lucifer realize what is going to happen in the end?

27. Seeing that Satan is very much real, and he is certainly not good. What should we do? How do we protect ourselves?

Find out more about JJ at journeywithjewels.wordpress.com and www.facebook.com/JJLiniger/.

For free stories, a sneak peek at new novels, and more, join the email list at JJLiniger.com and journeywithjewels@gmail.com

Enjoy a special preview of JJ's next novel, *God's Will.*

Sneak Preview Of God's Will

Prologue

Through all the sorrow and pain, joy and elation, he never doubted God's sovereign plan; that was, until today.

Reverend Daniel Peters sat in his car in front of the home of his dear friend Benjamin in shocked disbelief God would allow such intense tragedy to befall one family and so thoroughly tear them apart. The Reverend enjoyed breakfast each Tuesday morning with a collection of men. It was such a good time of laughter and learning few men in the group dared to miss it.

However, when Benjamin didn't show up last Tuesday, Peters whispered an urgent prayer for him and his young son. After another miss today, concern grew into panic as he repeatedly called his friend. Benjamin never answered, so the good Reverend found himself parked at the curb, praying for the courage to go inside.

Fearing the worst, Daniel exited his car and walked along the narrow path which led to the front door. He pressed the doorbell, heard it chime inside, and waited for a response. Silence. Not the usual sound of the news blaring on the T.V., or the playful sound of Benjamin's boy. The Reverend started calling the kid "Captain" after a church Halloween festival encouraged children to dress up as their favorite Disney character. The only part of the costume which authenticated the fictional Captain Jack Sparrow was the store-bought black braided wig. The rest was thrown together by borrowing his father's clothes. Peters called the boy 'Captain' and the nickname persisted to this day.

The Reverend waited a moment and then rang the doorbell again. Nothing.

His heart raced as he frantically pounded on the front door and called for his friend. "Benjamin! Benjamin! Captain!! It's me, Daniel!!"

The impact of his fist jarred the front door open. *Now what?* Peters listened for a response before walking in, and heard a muffled sound. Feeling relieved he may have found his friends, Peters listened harder. Voices changed, making him aware they belonged to the television.

Slowly he crept further inside. His eyes darted around the room searching for signs of life. He had been inside the home twice before in the past month to offer counsel to his friend. The home was as he remembered it. No obvious evidence of forced entry or burglary, which would help to explain Peter's feeling something terrible had happened here.

An odor similar to mold filled the air.

"Benjamin! Captain!" He made his way through the first floor, calling out to his friends.

As he ascended the staircase, the smell intensified, filling his nostrils with the aroma of rot and decay.

"Oh dear, Heavenly Father," he prayed aloud.

Once up the stairs, he followed the smell to the second door on the right. White knuckles twisted the door handle, and he looked inside. His heart pounded, and he heard his pulse echo behind his ears.

As the door swung open, his gaze concentrated on the floor to keep from seeing anything horrific. He caught the image of a large shadow looming in the doorway of the master bathroom. Reluctantly, he allowed his eyes to follow the shadow until he saw the disfigured corpse of his friend suspended above the ground. Flies and maggots had made a buffet of the bloated body, leaving behind the most horrific sight he had endured in over twenty years of ministry.

Bile rose to his throat which he swallowed down. As the reality of the moment sank into his soul, Peters suddenly remembered Benjamin's son. "Oh, sweet Jesus, where's Captain?" he prayed.

Peters sprinted from the room, stumbling down the hallways, and frantically searched for the lost boy. He dreaded finding another body. Room after room uncovered no one, and Peters realized there was something worse than discovering the dead body of a sweet kid.

What if he found nothing at all?

Thoughts raced through his mind. *Where was he?! Was he taken? Had he witness what happened to his father?*

Peters reached deep inside his soul and prayed, "God, I don't know where Captain is, but you do. Take him into your loving arms and protect him."

I hoped you enjoyed this sneak preview of JJ Liniger's next release. God's Will is scheduled to be released in February.

Find out more about JJ at journeywithjewels.wordpress.com and www.facebook.com/JJLiniger/.

ABOUT THE AUTHOR

JJ Liniger is the author of *Poisoned*, a mystery thriller. In the story, Trevor returns home after a thirteen-year absence to find Becton, Texas has become decimated. What happened?

JJ enjoys writing in multiple genres (thriller, romance, dystopian future, and young adult) which has led her to Indie publishing. She loves to read great books that allow her internal editor to become silent. Coffee pumps through her body as much as blood. She works hard to perfect the ability to write in a noisy and often messy home.

Find out more about JJ at journeywithjewels.wordpress.com and www.facebook.com/JJLiniger/.

For free stories, a sneak peek at new novels, and more, join the email list at JJLiniger.com and journeywithjewels@gmail.com.

Please take time to review. Thank You!

Made in the USA
Coppell, TX
27 December 2021